THE ONEDIN LINE

All, except Leonora, succeeded in grabbing the teak hand rail, but as she laughingly reached for her father's outstretched hand she found herself unaccountably floating away to pirouette, slowly at first, then faster and faster until, rotating like a top, she spun towards the open ladderway leading down to the maelstrom of the foredeck below. There was a wild howling in her ears, her bonnet whipped away from her head and her crinoline ballooned, tipping her forward until, wildly flailing the air, her feet left the deck and she found herself catapulted towards a nightmare of raging water.

THE ONEDIN LINE 4:
The Trade Winds

Cyril Abraham

A STAR BOOK
published by
the Paperback Division of
W. H. ALLEN & Co. Plc

A Star Book
Published in 1986
by the Paperback Division of
W. H. Allen & Co. Plc
44 Hill Street, London W1X 8LB

First published in Great Britain by
Tandem Publishing Ltd, 1977

Printed and bound in Great Britain by
Anchor Brendon Ltd, Tiptree, Essex

ISBN 0 352 32069 9

By arrangement with BBC Books, a division of
BBC Enterprises Ltd

The cover photograph shows Peter Gilmore as James Onedin from
the BBC-TV series *The Onedin Line*
BBC copyright © photograph John Green

For Bob and Dot

'I name this ship, Anne Onedin,*' pronounced Elizabeth, adding breathlessly: 'May God protect and preserve all who sail in her.'*

The bottle shattered against the stem. Champagne gushing and foaming, drenched her lilac dress with a wind-borne libation while the ladies clapped and cheered and the gentlemen yaw-haw-hawed and raised their top hats in acclamation.

For a moment the ship paused as though reluctant to leave the security of the land, then it trembled, shivered delicately and began to drift smoothly away from the edge of the gaily bedecked dais.

Slowly, then with gathering momentum, it slid down the greased slipway. A thunderous rumble shook the platform to its foundations and clouds of dust rose as the massive drag chains uncoiled to check the increasing rush of the ship to the sea. For one heart-stopping moment it seemed that the giant hull must plunge straight to the bottom. Then the stern swept the waters of the river into a miniature tidal wave sending a covey of small boats rocking and bobbing and the waiting tugs into a frenzy of hooting and tooting.

As the ship settled into her natural element James turned his bleak gaze upon Baines.

'She's all yours now, Captain,' he said, swung on his heel and walked away.

CHAPTER ONE

The *Anne Onedin* lay panting alongside the jetty in Bilbao, her iron sides drumming to the shake of crude ore pouring into the holds. Baines, leaning against the bridge rails, watched James trudging ashore and cursed the day he was ever given command of a steamship. He hated the ship. He hated the noisome clamour of the engine, the wild hiss of steam, and the all-pervading stench of grease and oil. Above all he hated the swirling black smoke that covered the decks in layers of grime and blew down his neck like the hot breath of Hades.

He turned his head as Albert emerged from the engine room like an apparition from the nether regions. His shirt, sleeves rolled to the elbow, was filthy, and his face streaked with grease and perspiration. He wiped his hands on a piece of dirty rag, saw Baines, waved cheerfully and sauntered amiably towards the bridge.

Northern Spain sweltered under a heatwave and choking red dust hung above the ship, turning the sun's brassy glare to a dull infernal glow.

'Good mornin', Captain,' Albert pronounced affably, as his head appeared above deck level. He stepped on to the bridge, fished a limp cigar from his pocket, stuck it between his teeth and perched himself on the rail beside Baines. He gestured towards the departing figure of James. 'I see our owner is off ashore again.'

'Ship's business,' grunted Baines uncommunicatively.

Albert patted his pockets, found a crushed matchbox and flared a light for his cigar. 'Anne's death took him hard,' he offered, seeking a conversational gambit.

Baines bit off a chaw of tobacco and spat over the side.

Albert tried again. 'They were as alike as two peas in a pod. I have never known anyone so affected by the death of a loved one.'

'They were close,' agreed Baines. 'Very close.'

'It is a pity she only left him a daughter. A son would have given him a sense of purpose.' An image of young William, now five years of age, stole into his mind. It was true, a son did lend purpose to ambition.

Baines' loyalty was affronted. 'I reckon Mr Onedin knows where he's going,' he stated huffily, and shifting the cud of tobacco ejected a stream of juice to arc through the air and splatter on the jetty thirty feet below.

Albert sighed. All his conversational gambits seemed to fall on deaf ears. Throughout the voyage James had been taciturn and morose, taking his meals in his cabin, emerging only to pace restlessly up and down the deck, black with thought. Baines, too, had been strangely resentful for a man richly rewarded with a plum command. Albert had eventually taken the hint and confined his activities to pottering around his beloved engine room, where at least he could indulge in conversation with Mr Longbotham, the chief engineer. Longbotham was a Lancashire man born and bred. A tall, gangling man of flat vowels and drawling speech who had learned his trade in the cotton mills of Bolton and had drifted to the Liverpool dockside in search of work.

Baines seemed to think it time to change the conversation. He jerked a thumb towards the ore rumbling into the holds. 'She'll roll like a sick pig,' he prophesied.

'I couldn't wish for a better cargo,' said Albert. 'It will test her under stress. We made a smooth passage out, never once had recourse to so much as a rag of canvas, engine turned sweetly and the patent steering engine has been beyond all expectation. But on the return voyage I think we should put her through her paces.' He broke off as Baines levered himself from the rails to glare at Albert with the air of a man who has suffered one indignity too many.

'Potato chopper!' he snarled. 'Damned potato chopper!' and hitching up his belt stalked majestically away to his quarters below the bridge.

Albert resignedly watched him go. Conversation on the return voyage promised to be at a premium.

Leaving the jetty, James paused to look back at the ship. Over Albert's protests she had been rigged as a three-masted barque with short pole masts, each with courses, single topsails and topgallants. She was a monster of a ship as ugly as sin with a straight stem and turtle deck aft. A tall blue and white funnel thrusting out of the midships housing lent her an ungainly cluttered look, rather like a floating warehouse with a factory chimney. But there was also a suggestion of brute strength, of raw elemental power harnessed to the will of man, a modern salamander born of fire and forged of iron.

He hailed a waiting carriage with a half-starved nag between the shafts and a half-asleep driver on the seat. In execrable Spanish he instructed the man to take him to the offices of Señor Perez, the local shipping agent, then sat back and lapsed into brooding silence.

The horse leaned tiredly into its harness and creaked forward slowly planting one splayed foot in front of the other as though testing an uncertain world for sureties. James tried to concentrate his thoughts, but as ever the past would intrude like a half-remembered pain, the ache returning in the restless maw of sleep, or the twisted chronology of time when he would hear an echo of her voice or catch a fugitive glimpse of a brown-skirted shade whisking away just beyond the periphery of his vision. At such times his brain seemed numb and the present was merely time to be filled with work, the future a series of stepping stones to be negotiated one at a time.

The Midas touch of the sun turned the river to gold and the narrow streets winding their way through a furnace of heat bouncing from white walls, seemed to scorch the very air he breathed. The carriage lurched over the cobblestones and eventually stopped outside a building of baked brick painted an eye-aching blue.

Inside, the office was cool, shaded from the glare of light by curtains of white lace swinging gently in a faint breeze to make shimmering watery patterns across the low ceiling.

Señor Perez greeted James with a limp moist hand, mopped his face with an enormous handkerchief, murmured the meaningless Spanish politeness 'my house is your house', and waved him to a cow-hide chair while one of the clerks pottered in with a jug of crushed limes and Seltzer water.

James allowed the cool liquid to trickle down his throat and waited patiently for Señor Perez to come to the point. He had a temperamental dislike of the Spanish custom of engaging in protracted civilities before arriving at the business in hand, but experience had taught him that interruptions served only to prolong the formalities. He therefore listened with only half an ear to the agent droning on about the weather, the state of the crops, the insolence of servants, the poverty of Spain compared with the wealth of England, and if Señor Onedin could find it in his heart to oblige his clients who were as poor as church mice he might be able to arrange a contract for the ships of Señor Onedin to carry regular cargoes of iron ore.

At which point James came out of his reverie and prepared for hard bargaining. Perez was, he knew, as astute as a cartload of monkeys and obviously wanted a fat commission from both ends. James wanted the highest freight charges he could squeeze, a twelve month contract with an option of renewal and no penalty clauses. The rules were as formalized as a game of chess. Inevitably they met in the middle and shook hands.

'There is one other little matter, Señor.' Perez beamed upon James and spread his arms like a man bearing gifts. 'I have also arranged for a number of passengers to accompany you to England.'

James heart sank at the prospect. Passengers were a necessary evil. They ate too much, drank too much, disturbed the peaceful routine of the ship, and imposed certain social obligations on the part of himself and Baines. On the other hand their money was good and the *Anne Onedin* had been built to accommodate up to twenty-five passengers. He took the proffered list and stuffed it into his pocket.

'I would ask that you afford every courtesy especially to Señor and Señora Bidolfo,' continued Perez. 'Señor Bidolfo is a personage of considerable influence and authority who has recently had the honour of gracing the table of His Excellency the Governor. He is paying ten English pounds in gold for the privilege of enjoying your finest accommodation.' He once again flourished his arms. 'I, myself, recommended the

Anne Onedin as the most magnificent vessel ever to sail from the port of Bilbao.'

James agreed with as good a grace as he could muster, haggled over the finer points of the contract, took his leave and set off back to the ship.

Bidolfo, he thought, as the carriage bumped and shook over the uneven cobblestones. Bidolfo sounded like some toffee-nosed Spanish grandee taking a sour visaged daughter on an educational tour of England. He would take care that the duty of entertainment fell to Baines' lot, after all he did speak their barbarous tongue like a native and one of the obligations of a master was to sit at table with the better class of passenger. James cheered up considerably at the prospect. With luck he should not only be able to avoid the passengers' company but also be able to take temporary command of the ship without unduly offending Baines' susceptibilities. The relationship between master and owner aboard the same ship was one that inevitably called for the exercise of tact, and to this end James had kept to himself as far as possible and steadfastly refused to proffer advice. Equally he had stood aside during the acrimonious disputes between Baines and Albert, Albert demanding a prolonged trial of his engine at maximum speed without regard for wind or sea, and Baines pleading to be allowed to hoist the sails. James had held his peace, calculated the saving in fuel costs, and been satisfied.

He paid off the driver, dodged beneath a basket of ore swinging at a derrick head, strode aboard and made his way to the saloon. With the noise of the steam winches hammering in his ears he stepped over the sill into the dimly lit interior and promptly fell over a small packing case. Hissing with the pain of a barked shin he sat up and began to curse roundly and luridly, only stopping in the midst of a choice epithet when he found himself staring into a pair of concerned brown eyes lowered to within a yard of his face.

The apparition wore a mantilla of white lace suspended from a high comb at the back of a rage of chestnut hair, and a white muslin dress, all frills and flounces, that cascaded down to a pair of tiny satin shoes. She had a pointed, elfin face with a wide mouth showing a row of even white teeth, and was small-boned and of almost doll-like fragility. James doubted her to be more than seventeen years of age, and from the deep golden tan of her skin concluded that she must be the Bidolfo daughter.

He bent his head and looked down at her from his height of six foot three.

'Seenyorita Beedolfo?' he asked in contorted Spanish.

Her mouth widened into an impish grin. She held out a lady-like hand. 'Con mucho gusto, Señor.'

James took the proffered hand, was about to give it a firm shake, then realized that he was expected to salute it in the continental fashion. He bent his head, cursing these foreign fripperies, and carefully pronounced his name. 'I am Onedin,' he told her. 'O-nee-din.'

'Nodeeyon?' she repeated, uncomprehending.

'O-nee-din,' he corrected, spelling it out slowly and raising his voice as though speaking to one bereft of the sense of hearing.

'Ony-o-din,' she exclaimed delightedly. 'Señor Ony-o-din, no es verdad?'

'It will do,' said James sourly. His eyes accustomed themselves to the gloom and he saw that the saloon was piled with luggage. A large travelling trunk, a couple of chests, a valise, a stack of suitcases and a mound of hatboxes, heaped and scattered in a disarray that offended his seaman's eye.

'I'll arrange to have your dunnage stowed in your staterooms,' he told her, turning to leave.

She put a finger to her chin and cocked her head. 'Que dice?'

He held out his hands and made a shooing motion. 'Momento. Wait – here – aquí.'

'Que pasa, Leonora?'

The voice came from the doorway and a shadow moved to stand in a shaft of yellow light streaming through one of the closed portholes. It was a tall man of down-turned lips and cold eyes in a bloodless face, and when he next spoke it was in the unmistakable flat accent of Lancashire. He held out a hand as white and limp as a dead fish.

'I'm Biddulph. I gather you've been making yourself acquainted with my daughter. You'll be Onedin, I take it?'

'I am,' said James, ignoring the hand. 'Perhaps you would be good enough to explain to Miss Biddulph that passengers are expected to confine themselves to their quarters until such time as the ship has completed taking on cargo.'

'Explain?' For a moment the man seemed nonplussed, then the thin banker's features broke into a doting parental smile. 'I am afraid Leonora has been teasing you, Mr Onedin. Spanish is her second language.'

The brown eyes tried to look contrite. 'Do forgive me, Mr Onedin,' she said. 'But I could not resist the temptation. You did look so helpless.'

There were those who could be amused at, or even take advantage of such a situation, but James was not of their number. He swallowed his anger and spoke coldly to her father. 'You will please inform your daughter that a ship is not a kindergarten, and that the commands of her officers are to be obeyed at all times.' Swinging on his heel he stalked away with as much dignity as he could muster and a half-suppressed splutter of feminine laughter burning his ears.

Three days later the *Anne Onedin* slipped down the Nervion river as an apricot sky heralded the approach of dawn. Turning her back on the bare brown hills of Spain the ship met the first long rollers of the Bay and, with her screw churning the sea into a private river of foam, bore away for the long haul to Ushant.

CHAPTER TWO

The heatwave which held Spain in its furnace grip stretched fiery fingers as far north as Scotland and drenched the cool hills and vales of England with a blaze of light. The cities were cauldrons, with air almost too parched to breathe; the inhabitants broiled indoors or baked outside; horses drooped miserably between the shafts of their carts; the river flowed like oil and the sailing ships lay helplessly at anchor with sails hanging limp and motionless while the busy ferryboats fulminated from shore to shore and deep-laden steamships brayed triumph from throaty whistles.

Not a shred of cloud disturbed the endless blue of the sky as Elizabeth walked William through the park. The child wore a velvet sailor suit and seemed totally unaffected by the oppressive heat. He ran ahead on little chubby legs and startled a drowsing pigeon out of its wits by clapping his hands and whoo-hooing at the top of his voice then returned obediently to his mother's command.

They strolled hand in hand along the tree-shaded path, paused at the lake to feed the ducks and listen to the bandsmen, boiling in blue brass-buttoned uniforms, blaring martial music to a group of gossiping nursemaids and a perspiring park keeper, before moving on to watch the Punch-and-Judy show.

There was a small crowd congregated before the red-and-white striped box and Mr Punch was squawking, 'Take that, take that!' as he belaboured the unfortunate Mrs Punch with his cudgel while the dog, Toby, sat and yawned and scratched at a flea behind her ruffled neck.

'I can't see, mama,' William complained and danced up and down as though on springs.

Elizabeth folded her parasol and stooped to lift him when a well-remembered voice said: 'I'll take him. Up you go, young fellow-me-lad.'

Daniel Fogarty swept the child high into the air and perched him upon his shoulder while her heart, that notorious thief of the affections, stumbled towards her throat and her face burned hotter than a thousand suns. To hide her confusion she opened and twirled her parasol.

'Are you keeping well, Elizabeth?' he inquired politely. 'This is indeed an unexpected pleasure.'

'I am of excellent health, thank you, Mr Fogarty,' she replied with equal formality.

His laugh boomed out above the shrieks of Mrs Punch and heads turned as he held the child crowing with delight at the full stretch of his arms.

'Your mother is a stickler for the proprieties, isn't she, my little macaroni? But I have a fancy that you, my fine gentleman, take after your uncle Daniel. Isn't that so?' and bringing the boy down to within an inch of his bearded face, peered into the deep sable eyes so much like his own.

The child stared back solemnly for a moment then gurgled: 'Uncle Dan'l. Lift me up again, Uncle Dan'l, lift me up.'

'Be careful, Daniel,' warned Elizabeth.

He grinned at her, 'I shan't drop him. He's too precious a bundle for that. Aren't you, son?'

She bit her lip. 'I didn't mean that. I meant, guard your tongue. He's quite the little chatterbox.'

'Of course he is,' roared Daniel, whirling the boy above his head once again. 'He's a chip off the old block, aren't you, little man?' He grinned at her and winked impudently.

Leading them away from the gaze of the curious and thereby drawing a wail of disappointment from William, she gathered her wits and eyed Daniel with a sly sidelong glance. He was too bumptious by far and in need of taking down a peg or two. They walked on a little way and turned off into a secluded arbour of grassy banks and carefully tended shrubs. The sun dappled the leaves of an oak carved with the names of long-forgotten lovers and insects hummed and sang, filling the drowsy stillness with their ancient busy music.

Daniel lowered William to the ground and together they watched the boy scrampering after a golden-winged butterfly. He took one of her gloved hands in his. 'I've missed you, Elizabeth,' he said softly.

She withdrew her hand and stepped back a pace. 'And how is dear Emma?' she asked with distant politeness. 'We see little of her these days.'

He had the grace to look embarrassed. A flush darkened his features and for a moment he was the old, awkwardly shy Daniel of so long, long ago.

'She is showing considerable improvement,' he replied with equal formality. 'Her melancholia is less apparent, although she still tends to keep herself in seclusion.'

'Emma was never of robust disposition,' she told him, and looking at his troubled face found difficulty in keeping her voice cool and level. 'Really, Daniel, I sometimes think you have no consideration for the sensibilities of others. How could you have permitted so fragile a creature to embark upon so long a voyage?'

'It was her father's wish,' he said defensively. He shuffled his feet again and stared morosely at his toes. 'And Emma was by no means averse to the suggestion. I am afraid she had somewhat fanciful notions as to the romaticism of the sea, and by the time she discovered her error it was too late. There were times when I quite feared for her reason.'

She moved away, putting a further distance between them, remembering Emma as she had stepped off the ship. She had eyes like frightened mice and had stood on the quay, swaying slightly and smiling vacantly as though unaware of her surroundings. Elizabeth, in spite of a pang of jealousy, had felt quite sorry for her and had hurried forward to offer a warm welcome, but Emma had swept past without a flicker of recognition to board her waiting carriage and drive away without so much as a by-your-leave.

'Mr Callon took it hard, very hard,' Daniel was saying.

Elizabeth came out of her reverie. 'His health is improving, I trust?'

Daniel shook his head. 'He is sinking. Sinking fast, I am afraid.'

The boy strutted back, marching to the sound of invisible drums. 'Come, William,' she said, taking his hand. 'It is time to leave. Say goodbye to Uncle Daniel.'

'Goodbye, Uncle Dan'l,' he said obediently. 'Why don't you ask Mama if you can call one day?'

Daniel looked at her quizzically and she mouthed 'Don't you dare!' But her eyes had filled with laughter and he thought he detected a hint of temptation buried in their depths.

She gave him a bewitching smile. 'Goodbye, Daniel,' she said and walked the child away.

As they turned the corner and disappeared from view he heard the childish treble piping above the fluting of a bird. 'I like Uncle Dan'l, Mama. I like Uncle Dan'l a lot,' adding with the indefatigable optimism of childhood: 'Why can't Uncle Dan'l come and stay with us while Papa is away?'

He did not hear her reply, but smiled ruefully to himself at the thought of so dazzling a possibility. He allowed a decent interval to elapse then sauntered out, a staid, well-dressed English gentleman escaping the cares of business with an afternoon stroll in the park. Turning his steps towards the park gates, his mind seething with discontent, he drifted rather than walked with any sense of purpose in the direction of Callon's gloomy mansion. He had come to hate the house which, sheltered from the gaze of the vulgar by a high surrounding wall topped by rows of poplars, lurked at the head of a driveway that wound through banks of moulting shrubbery with gnarled roots and dusty leaves wilting in the torpid air.

Trudging up the path, the gravel crunching beneath his feet like the dried bones of dead ambitions, he thought once again how the house reminded him of a great stone mausoleum. The huge iron-studded door looked as though it had been designed to seal its inhabitants in rather than keep out intruders. He jerked at the bell-pull and the answering bell jangled like a knell from a distant cavern.

The door swung open and Mrs Crowther, their aged housekeeper, sandy wig askew and reeking of mothballs, blinked recognition from short-sighted eyes before stepping aside to usher him into a long dark hall panelled with oak and raftered with antiquity.

The house was built of blocks of quarried sandstone and, in spite of the torrid temperature outside, was as cool and dank as a tomb. He made his way into the library, poured himself a large tot of brandy and sprawled broodingly in a deep leather armchair. The library was walled with unread books, and the tall mullioned windows seemed designed to trap the darkness rather than let in light. The empty fireplace sighed behind its embroidered firescreen and Callon's portrait in mayoral robes stared across an eternity of time.

Daniel sipped his brandy while images of memory flickered like fireflies behind his shuttered eyelids. In a few short years he had come a long way from being mate of a brigantine, but success seemed to have turned to ashes. Callon lay upstairs, croaking out his life in the big fourposter bed; Emma wandered the house like a wraith, haunted with terror, twitching at shadows and muttering incomprehensibilities. Soon, perhaps within days, Callon would die, and then the entire responsibilities of the business would devolve upon his shoulders. He shivered at the thought and reached once again for the solace of the brandy decanter. The fact was that office management remained a mystery to him; he had never had a head for finance, and the multifarious activities of a shipping company were as far beyond his comprehension as calculus to a Hottentot. His natural element was the deck of a ship. He could handle a ship, and he could handle men, and sail across the snarling seas of the world with the confident arrogance of his kind, but always at the bidding of the owner.

He sat, rolling the brandy around his tongue, mulling over the past and wishing to God he was back aboard a ship, when suddenly the recollection of the chance meeting flared into his mind like a falling star. He remembered again the surge of his blood, the knot of anguish tightening in the pit of his stomach at the sight of the boy, young and sturdy with his own dark hair and dark eyes, and wondered yet again how she could possibly have chosen to marry Albert, that strutting, mincing nincompoop. Tormented by the defeated lover's eternal cry 'If only. . . . If only,' he gulped down his brandy while the house stirred restlessly as though emerging from a long sleep.

He heard, only half aware, muted voices and pattering footsteps, the swish of a gown and a far away distant keening like the cry of a wounded bird, while his inner ear repeated the child's piping voice: 'I like Uncle Dan'l' and, 'Mama, why can't Uncle Dan'l come and stay with us?' while Elizabeth's features swam before him until even her perfume seemed to fill the room.

The door swung open and Emma stood framed against the greater darkness of the hall, her wide crinoline and statuesque stillness giving the momentary illusion of a life-size portrait by a Dutch master.

Still inflamed with memory he stared sullenly at this disturber of his dreams until she moved and he saw the tear-stained face.

'It's Papa,' she said. 'He is asking for you.'

He took the stairs two at a time and hurried into the vast bedroom with the great canopied bed and the smell of death hanging like an obscene incense. The curtains were drawn to keep out the heat of the day and candle flames guttered on their wicks. Callon lay beneath a mound of bedclothes, his empty stare-eye glittering vacantly at the ceiling, his breath rasping the silence like the slow surge of a distant tide. Then the other eye opened, roved and probed the shadows to gleam with recognition as it lit upon Daniel.

The shrunken features, bagged with decaying flesh, twisted into the grimace of a smile and Daniel bent his head to listen to the words whistling from the labouring throat.

'I'm done for, Daniel,' said Callon. 'I'm off to meet me Maker.' The grotesque grin twitched in a semblance of the old cantankerous style. 'And not before time. I've a word or two of argument for His ear, though I doubt He will pay as little heed in heaven as He did on earth.' His hand scrabbled across the coverlet like a strange scaley insect to grip Daniel's finger with surprising strength. The voice became an urgent whisper. 'Take care of Emma. Promise, Daniel, promise.'

'I promise,' said Daniel. He turned his head to find Emma weeping softly at his side. 'I promise,' he said again.

The grip tightened. 'You've always been a son to me, Daniel. Everything will be yours. It's all there, signed and sealed.' The solitary eye swivelled in its socket directing Daniel's gaze to a scroll of parchment lying amid an array of medicine bottles on the bedside table. 'Keep the name of the Company, and bow to no man.'

'I promise,' reiterated Daniel.

'I'm hauling down my flag now.' The voice whispered to a long drawnout sigh and was still.

Daniel looked down at the crumped face and realized that he was crying. Tears scalded his eyes and coursed down his cheeks to saturate his beard in salty benediction. He had always loved the old man, loved him for his stubborn will, his pride, his fierce independence, his sudden rages and equally sudden lapses into coarse humour. He had been a gruff tyrant to his employees, but kindness itself to Daniel.

He put an arm about Emma's shoulders and found for once she did not shudder at his touch. Instead she nestled her head against his chest and gave way to a paroxysm of grief while her father's sightless gaze remained fixed upon an eternity of defiance.

Daniel released the cold hand and gently drew the sheets over the quiet face. Suddenly he realized that he was now Callon and Company and felt more alone at that moment than he had ever been in his life before. He hugged Emma towards him as though seeking a prop for his life, and remembering his promise, sought clumsily for words of solace.

'It will be all right, Emma,' he mumbled. 'I shall take care of you.'

The deep violet eyes raised to meet his, and for a moment she stared at him like a child lost in wonder. Then she pulled away to moan and shake her head, wagging it from side to side as though trying to rid herself of an intolerable burden.

'No! No, no, no!' she wailed, and to his consternation began to laugh with a wild hysteria that turned the house into a bedlam of lunatic shrieks and raised the hairs at the nape of his neck.

He reached out to shake her into some semblance of sanity but she backed away even further, stretched her hands like claws and spat at him.

'Never!' she screeched. 'Never, never, never!' Then, crinoline billowing, raven black hair streaming in disarray, she fled from the room. Her demented cries echoed and re-echoed along the corridor until the slam of her door left him alone and the house once more wrapped him in its silence.

He stood looking down at the shape lying beneath the bedclothes and wished himself ten thousand miles away. And the wish, as though conjured by some protective demon, burgeoned, took shape, startled him with its sudden clarity.

'Why not?' he thought. 'By God, why not!'

CHAPTER THREE

Loaded to the gunwales with two thousand tons of iron ore, the *Anne Onedin* headed north and west across Biscay, rolling sluggishly in the deep ocean swell.

For the first couple of days the passengers remained in the confines of their cabins, and James took quiet satisfaction from the moans and groans issuing from Mr Biddulph's stateroom.

On the third day, however, with the sun burning a hole in a cerulean blue sky, little Miss Biddulph emerged looking pale but determined. She lunched with Baines and Albert, but spoke little, concentrating solely on the food set before her.

By dinner time, however, aided by the resilience of youth, she had fully recovered and ate with the appetite of a young savage. She had also recovered the use of her tongue and prattled away happily on the first topic that took her fancy, rarely waiting for a reply before moving to the next subject. Baines was delighted and Albert quietly amused by her conversational vivacity, but to James she had become an intolerable pest disturbing his solitary musings by constantly appearing at his shoulder with a stream of inconsequential questions. How long was the ship? How broad? How deep? Did Mr Onedin own many ships? Her father owned several collieries in Lancashire, and they lived in a simply enormous mansion with dozens of rooms and hordes of servants, and poor Mama died not long after she was born and was Mr Onedin married?

James, his head aching abominably from her incessant chatter, had finally escaped to the sanctuary of his quarters, there to brood over the one piece of useful information he had been able to glean from her vapourings: Biddulph was a mine owner, and coal and ships went together like hay and horses; steamships devoured mountains of coal, and sailing ships freighted it as cargo to distant coaling stations. Biddulph, therefore, might be worth the trouble of cultivating.

A day later Biddulph finally emerged looking, according to a grinning Baines, for all the world like a sick tortoise. He took a little broth and remained uncommunicative for the rest of the day. But the following morning, with the *Anne Onedin* pitching towards Ushant, his querulous voice could be heard raised in the forerunner of many plaints. The ship, he announced to all and sundry, was dangerously overloaded, so much so that even in the calmest of weather it pitched and rolled beyond all reason. A body had merely to step down to the lower deck to invite being washed overboard.

James had listened, gritted his teeth and, forgetting his promise to cultivate the fool, had asked acidly if he would appreciate free advice on the hewing of coal?

Choking with rage Biddulph had next tackled Captain Baines. But that worthy had simply creased his features into a broad grin and promptly launched into a series of reminiscences about the horrors of life aboard Western Ocean packet ships.

'You are the luckiest of men,' Baines had concluded, clapping him on the back with quite uncalled for familiarity. 'First rate accommodation, choice victuals three times a day, a short voyage and the Bay as smooth as glass.'

Biddulph had snarled disagreement. The accommodation fell far below the standard he had been led to believe, it was cramped, uncomfortable and over-priced; the service was poor and the food inedible; moreover the behaviour and disgusting language of the crew was deplorable. He would have continued further but Miss Biddulph had intervened to remark that she trusted dear Captain Baines and Mr Onedin utterly, and that Mr Onedin, as anyone with half an eye could see, was a man of principle, sterling character, and unassailable integrity.

Biddulph had given up. He could not for the life of him begin to comprehend his daughter's motiveless attachment to a man whom he considered to be taciturn and boorish to the point of rudeness. Chewing on an unlighted cigar and shaking his head in despair at the female temperament, he had come to the conclusion that Leonora was fast approaching an age when a suitable match must be found. As an only child she would be heiress to a considerable fortune and suitors would soon be buzzing around like wasps around a honey pot. The last thing he wanted was to find her impressionable head turned by some languid ne'er-do-well with a taste for the gaming tables.

Leonora had privately come to much the same conclusion. She was almost eighteen, an age at which most of her contemporaries had long since settled into a comfortable marital status, and was shrewdly aware that most marriages, far from being made in heaven, were more often than not arranged in the more prosaic surroundings of boardrooms and gentlemen's clubs. On the other hand she had not the slightest intention of allowing herself to be married off to some gouty old lobster with an office in the City and one foot in the grave. She would choose with care, she decided, and had taken to examining James with a speculative eye as he took his solitary constitutional along the weather side of the boatdeck.

The ship pushed the sea aside and wallowed towards a smudge of land, a rocky island outpost thrusting into the Atlantic.

'Ushant,' said James briefly, snapping the telescope shut.

Baines grunted agreement and stepped off the distance on the chart. 'I make it about twenty miles off.'

For a moment Ushant light mirrored the sun and flashed a searing warning across the endless slopes of the sea. A tug of wind suddenly set the bridge awning to snapping and flapping. With the ingrained habit of a lifetime they turned their heads in unison to face the change of wind direction. To the west the sun seemed to have been nailed to the sky by an omnipotent hand, while below it the first of the storm clouds began to wash the horizon in streaks of glowing colour.

James glanced away and towards the distant menace of Ushant. 'We'd best turn and face it,' he said.

Baines scraped a hand across his chin and cast a measuring glance at the long rollers sliding in from the Atlantic, each imperceptibly larger than its forerunner. He shook his head decisively. 'Not yet. We'll batten down first. Once we turn into a head sea they'll be coming over green.'

James nodded assent, and walked to the engine room voice pipe. 'Carry on, Captain Baines,' he said formally. 'I'll alert the engineer.'

Painted white, the iron walls of the engine room rose high towards the cathedral vault of the skylights. Over all was the unmistakable, all-pervading smell of hot metal and oil mingling with mists of steam from swollen pipes and pounding machinery. The enormous crank-heads and connecting rods rose and fell, the propeller shaft hummed smoothly, gleaming in the reflected light of swinging oil lamps. The pot-bellied low-pressure cylinder gasped wheezingly at every thrust of the pistons while the needles of pressure gauges asked and answered their own flickering questions.

Mr Longbotham moved easily along iron platforms slippery with oil and grease. Unaffected by the boom of the sea and the sluggish roll of the ship, he threaded his way between flailing metal arms and eccentrically rotating discs, checking grease boxes and dribbling oil over the clattering, big-jointed connecting rods. Long practice had filtered out the concomitant din so that his hearing was attuned to every nuance of the machinery roaring and thundering about his head. Alert for the slightest sound of discordance he easily picked out the soft whistle of the voice pipe. Scuttling along the galleries and sliding down the short flights of iron steps like an animated crab, he made his way to the control platform where the wide gaping mouth of the speaking tube and the large half-dial of the engine room telegraph with its stubby black finger pointing resolutely to FULL AHEAD, were affixed to the stokehold bulkhead.

Longbotham removed the whistle, pronounced 'Hullo?', and put his ear to the bell-mouth.

'We are in for a blow,' said a disembodied voice. 'We'll be shutting down to half speed in about twenty minutes.'

Longbotham eyed the pressure gauges and swore softly to himself. 'Very well, if tha says so,' he replied. 'But us'll need to blow off a pound or two of steam.'

Without waiting for a reply he replaced the mouthpiece and dropped down the ladder to the floor. Swinging open the big iron door he released a blast of heat and stepped through into the stokehold. The crescendo of the engine died away to a muffled thudding as the door closed behind him and he took a moment or two to adjust his vision to the blood-red gloom.

Half-naked demonic figures toiling at the task of feeding the fires of Hell, paused to stare at this intrusion into their private world of torment. White teeth gleamed and white eyes rolled in grotesque masks of dust and sweat then, chests heaving, breath rasping in parched throats, they again stooped and staggered at their eternal labour. Shovels scraped across the iron floor to scoop heaps of coal from the waiting hoppers and hurl the contents into the gaping mouths of the open fire boxes. The fires roared and licked yellow serpent-tongues of flame into the darkness. The ship swayed and rolled, and avalanches of coal slid across a slope of iron.

It was a pit of hell lying in the bowels of the ship. Three scarcely human skeletons tended six fires. Two laboured at the mounds of coal, while the third heaved at a long iron slice bar, jabbing and raking at glowing clinkers and tumbling the detritus into the ash pits below the howling furnaces.

The donkeyman, a tall ramrod of a man with a tight overseer's face, emerged from his lair beneath the ash chute which, reaching to the main deck far above, allowed a draught of cooler air to enter the stokehold.

'We 'as a full 'ead o' steam, sir,' he announced in the flat adenoidal accents of Liverpool.

Longbotham nodded approval and cast a glance at the needles of the pressure gauges hovering at the red 60 lbs per square inch mark.

'Tha's done very well, Donkey,' he said. 'Very well, indeed. But we'll have to damp down – and tha'd best draw number three fire into the bargain, she's choked to her gullet wi' ash.'

The donkeyman stared in disbelief. 'Damp down? Now? Dammit all, we've not long since raised a full head!' He began to curse, rapidly and fluently, while behind him the coal-black demons leaned on their shovels and grinned appreciation.

Longbotham jerked a thumb. 'Orders from above,' he said, and reaching over his head hauled down on the whistle lanyard until the gauges dropped to a matching fifty pounds. Even here, twenty feet below the waterline, they could hear the first throaty gurgle of the whistle followed by the harsh, long-drawn rasp of escaping steam.

Resignedly the firemen kicked shut the firedoors and lowered the huge iron dampers, while within the furnaces the fires died to a dull angry glow.

Longbotham paused before re-opening the engine room door and eyed the exhausted black gang encouragingly.

'Steady yourselves, lads,' he told them. 'We're in for a tossing.'

The passengers had found their sea legs and were taking a post-prandial promenade, occasionally staggering from side to side like drunken marionettes as the long slow roll of the ship canted the deck away from uncertain feet. The sudden snarl and gush of steam from the whistle stopped them in their tracks as though jerked by invisible wires, and their heads turned in unison to stare at the phenomenon as though only by a prolonged examination of the texture and quality of the steam could they arrive at a resolution of the cause.

As the snore died away to a whispering flutter and then ceased altogether, Biddulph, who had noticed that the seamen going about their work had paid but scant attention to the uproar, cleared his throat and coughed authoritatively.

'There is no cause for alarm, ladies and gentlemen,' he pronounced. 'It is no more than the operation of the boiler's safety valve allowing surplus steam to escape. I assure you that without such a device we should all be blown to smithereens.' His crocodile features twisted into a self-congratulatory grin.

'You are versed in such matters, sir?' asked Major Hendricks. The major was a short, stubby man who seemed to have been exploded into a tight-fitting uniform of red and blue with gold facings and was invariably accompanied by his wife, a prim stiff-necked lady with a face like a closed purse.

'Coal is my business, sir,' replied Biddulph. 'And I think I may lay fair claim to a rudimentary knowledge of things mechanical.' He pointed to the tenuous clouds of steam flowing away before a rapidly freshening breeze. 'That, sir, represents nothing other than waste, sheer waste. With coal fetching fifteen shillings a ton it would appear that someone has, quite literally, money to burn.'

Thus reassured the group continued their interrupted perambulation while the seamen lashed down the lifeboats, turned the engine room ventilators back to wind, removed the cowls from the remaining ventilators and plugged the shafts, the carpenter and his mate methodically hammered home the wedges in the hatch coamings, and the ship, battened down tight and snug, waited to do battle with its old enemy, the sea.

Leonora, laughing, made a little skipping run as the wind, billowing her crinoline into a miniature sail, trundled her along the deck as though on wheels until she brought up with a crash against the after rail. She expelled a cheerful 'whoosh' and then pointed with the ferrule of her folded parasol towards the horizon.

'What a pretty sky!' she exclaimed.

They agreed that it was, indeed, a pretty sky and admiringly contemplated long tendrils of copper-hued cloud spreading across the western horizon. Beneath the cloud the sea sparkled green and gold with a faint line of creamy froth, like milk beginning to simmer in a vast saucer.

'Quite magnificent, my dear,' Biddulph concurred, adding as an explanatory note to the uninitiated: 'It is only at sea that one can fully appreciate the grandiloquent design of the Almighty. Ashore, one's view is necessarily restricted by buildings and the smoke from the chimneys of our manufacturies.'

Mrs Hendricks begged leave to differ. 'In Delhi, where Major Hendricks was stationed for many years, we were often privileged to witness some of the most glorious manifestations of a benign Providence it were possible to imagine. Is that not so, Major?'

Major Hendricks blew agreement through his sandy moustache. 'Absolutely. Pack o' heathens, all of 'em, but sunsets first class, I'll not deny.'

They balanced on the heaving deck and watched enthralled as the clouds spun crimson webs across an indigo sky, while beyond the distant rim of the horizon the sea began to froth and boil as the deep Atlantic rollers were flayed into sheets of foam by the power of a wind that had raged unchecked across a thousand miles of ocean.

'I do believe we are changing direction,' remarked Mrs Hendricks conversationally, and looked to Biddulph, the self-appointed expert, for explanation.

Fascinated they watched the line of clouds dance across the horizon as though in time to an invisible orchestration and then stop abruptly right ahead of the ship.

'Seem to be heading straight into it, what?' commented the Major. 'Odd, deuced odd. Must have made a right-angled turn.'

Biddulph pursed his lips. 'Quite, quite. I imagine that our present course would have brought us rather too close to the land for safety. A fact which in no way surprises me. I may say that I am by no means satisfied with the manner in which the affairs of this ship are conducted.'

Mrs Hendricks, who had bivouacked on the plains of India and considered shipboard life a luxury rather than a hardship, took leave to suggest that as the owner was aboard Mr Biddulph should more correctly address his complaints to him.

'I have, Madam,' Biddulph replied tartly. 'The man is a boor.'

The first sea broke over the bows sending twin fans of spray cascading across the foredeck, the ship's head rose high in the air, paused for a moment suspended between sky and water, then plunged thunderously into the trough below. The propeller lifted clear to thrash madly while the engine hammered under the strain. Then the stern dipped, the propeller bit into the sea and the engine settled back into its rhythmic poundings as the ship lurched, shouldered aside a second mountain of water, shook herself angrily, and tossed a rainbow of spume into the sky.

The passengers clung to the rails and stared in wonder at a plumed army of waves marching across the horizon beneath tattered banners of cloud.

'Water seems a little choppy, what?' ventured Major Hendricks as the ship, rolling tipsily, allowed a sea to slop over the gunwales and run playfully along the foredeck.

'Perhaps we should retire to our quarters?' Mrs Hendricks suggested nervously. 'I do believe the weather is taking a turn for the worse.'

The shrill bugle call of the wind lent emphasis to her words, and they turned to make their staggering way back to their accommodation when the storm struck like a fist.

All, except Leonora, succeeded in grabbing the teak hand rail, but as she laughingly reached for her father's outstretched hand she found herself unaccountably floating away to pirouette, slowly at first, then faster and faster until, rotating like a top, she spun towards the open ladderway leading down to the maelstrom of the foredeck below. There was a wild howling in her ears, her bonnet whipped away from her head and her crinoline ballooned, tipping her forward until, wildly flailing the air, her feet left the deck and she found herself catapulted towards a nightmare of raging water.

A sea broke over the bulwarks, sweeping all before it and engulfing Leonora's falling body in a roaring smother of foam. It raised her high before hammering her to the deck with a force that drove the breath from her lungs, then it tumbled her over and over like a rag doll, plucking at her clothes and pulling at arms and limbs as though bent on tearing her apart. Then the ship's head plunged and the turbulent weight of water released its grasp to draw back, snarling and champing along the deck.

She struggled spluttering to her feet, dazed and wild-eyed with terror, only to see a second green wall towering above her head. As she opened her mouth in a soundless scream an arm wrapped itself about her waist and a voice spoke sharply in her ear: 'Save your breath. And don't struggle.'

Leonora just had time to catch a glimpse of a lean face grinning encouragement before the mountain of water thundered to the deck and she found herself once again kicking and struggling and fighting for breath.

In obedience to his command she had drawn in a quick breath and clamped her lips tight shut, but the sea squeezed and pummelled and swung her this way and that until, head pounding and lungs bursting, she could endure no longer and opened her mouth. Bitter-tasting salt water forced its way down her throat. She retched and swallowed and retched again while a world of ice-cold water surged and roared about her and sought to pound the life from her body. She began to claw at the restraining arm, fighting to free herself that she might rise to the surface and the life-giving air above. But the grip merely tightened and she came to the panic conclusion that the monster was trying to drown her. She kicked out weakly then, as her head seemed ready to explode, she suddenly saw clouds racing across a wheeling sky. Darts of pain thrust through her chest as, in most unladylike fashion, she spewed out a mouthful of vomit and water, before gulping in a lungful of the sweetest air she had ever tasted.

James unlocked his arm from the stanchion of the ladder to which he had anchored himself and dragged the bedraggled, half-conscious, Leonora to the lower steps. A bearded seaman leaped catlike to the deck and together they carried her, coughing and spluttering, to the sanctury of the boatdeck above.

'Take her below,' said James, and turned his attention to a world gone mad.

The wind howled out of a black sky and white spume tore from the tops of waves rolling in like steep green cliffs. The ship bucked and tossed and fought the sea, while down below the firemen staggered and swore and one of their number screamed as he was flung against the hot boiler plates and the skin bubbled like tar and stripped from his back. In the engine room the air was warm and sticky and the groan of the ship, shuddering under the stunning blows of the sea, added a deep dull note to the roar and stammer of the engine.

Longbotham stood on the control platform, his arms raised as though in prayer as his hands gripped the rim of a wheel protruding at an angle above his head. Whenever the ship pitched he would check the engine's racing by screwing hard at the wheel, while below him the second engineer waited patiently at the controls of the starting gear. The third engineer had already disappeared into the shaft tunnel on a tour of examination. The oil lamps danced and swung crazily, casting leaping skeletal shadows on the white-painted bulkheads, while the ventilators hummed and moaned like giant organ pipes as the air rushed in and out in the backwash of the wind.

In the tunnel the bearings screamed and smoked as the enormous cylindrical shaft whirred and sang. There was barely enough room for a stooping man, and even then it was necessary to move sideways. Mr Morgan, the third engineer, shuffling along towards the stern tube, crouched over his task of spooning black grease into the bearing boxes. It was a job he hated. A knot of fear twisted in the pit of his stomach at every rush of the sea, and the further he moved from the engine room the more his terror increased. The tunnel was an arched semicircle hooped with iron and echoing to the thrum of the spinning shaft. The shaft, eighteen inches in diameter, almost five feet in circumference and thirty feet in length, was supported on iron cradles and ran on curved arms holding the plummer blocks.

Morgan bowed over his work, stooping and shuffling until he

reached the stern tube through which the shaft disappeared into the turbulent sea beyond. It passed through a massive bush machined into a series of grooves containing blocks of lignum vitae. As the bearings were lubricated by the action of sea-water there was always a slight seepage which trickled into the bilges to be dealt with by the pumps. But the clammy touch of the metal plates and the sight of the sea squeezing through as though from a sponge invariably raised the hair on the nape of Morgan's neck.

He set his teeth and bent lower to make his last check before scurrying back to the security of the engine room.

The propeller consisted of four blades of phosphor bronze riveted to a central boss. The constant uneven pounding had so weakened one blade that it had begun to curl and feather at the edges and each succeeding chop into the sea sent tremors and vibrations throughout its length.

Once again the bows plunged, shaking the stern clear of the water. The screw thrashed wildly, the stern plummeted and the propeller blade, tearing itself free of the boss, was struck by its rotating companion with the transmitted force of three thousand horse power. It sheared off leaving a short stub to revolve with the remaining pair of blades in an increasingly eccentric orbit. The torque on the solid iron shaft increased and it began to wobble and grind horribly.

Morgan turned and ran, white-faced, the length of the tunnel, expecting at any moment the shaft to bend like a hairpin until it snapped in the middle to flail like a giant arm, smashing everything in its path and mangling him to rags. The breath scorched in his lungs as he tried to scream a warning above the roar of the machinery. The stern lifted and tilted and crashed yet again into the sea with a bone-shaking jar that reverberated throughout the ship and drove the engine to a fresh paroxysm of chattering anger. A rat ran over his feet squeaking alarm and he kicked out wildly at the furry body before erupting into the engine room and clawing his way to the control platform and the calm figure of Longbotham. He tried to gasp out his message and only then realized that he might as well have saved his breath, for the engine was already stuttering to a halt and Longbotham was turning his head to speak urgently into the voice pipe.

On the bridge Baines listened incredulously, while all around him the seas raged, and the dipping sun set the western horizon aflame. He looked over his shoulder to where Ushant light, high on its rocky perch, winked a yellow eye and searched the sky with a scything beam.

'You've got to give us time,' he yelled into the mouthpiece, and bent his ear to listen to the gargling reply. He replaced the whistle and straightened up to find James standing at his shoulder.

'They say we've got to heave-to,' he exploded. 'Heave-to! In this! Blasted engines!' he swore. 'Damned devil contraptions!'

James balanced easily against the rise and fall of the deck. 'You have had a hankering to make sail ever since we left port. This would seem to be your opportunity.' He steadied himself against a howling blast of wind and went to the voice pipe 'How long can you give us?' he asked, listened, then: 'Ah – it is you, Albert? Think yourself fortunate that I did not take your advice and build a ship without provision for sails. Yes, Albert, I am sure you are right – but that day has not yet dawned. You must keep that engine turning until you hear from us. Very well.' He turned to face Baines. 'We have about ten minutes. Mr Albert has taken charge.'

'Mr Prentiss!' roared Baines, and the second mate, huddled unhappily on the weather wing of the bridge, came to life and hurried forward.

'Roust 'em out, Mr Prentiss. All hands to make sail. Smartly now. Jump to it, young man,' snapped Baines as a black mountain burst over the bows to sweep the foredeck in an avalanche of water that seethed and foamed over hatches and winches. The explosion of spray reached high above the bridge to be whirled away by the wind in a hissing rainstorm that turned to steam as it lashed into the hot funnel casing.

James ducked his head, buried his chin in his coat collar, then returned his gaze to a speculative measurement of the distance between the ship and Ushant's raking light, now no more than ten miles off the quarter.

'We'd better make a run for it,' he suggested, trying to keep the edge of command from his voice.

Baines raised his head, sniffing the air like an animal casting for a scent. 'Wind's backing. She'll blow herself out soon.' He hoisted the cud of tobacco into his other cheek. 'Hove-to, we might make it. Bring her round, and we'll broach for sure.'

Ushant light cut swathes of cloud from the sky. James shook his head decisively. 'The wind and sea would pile us up. We'll take our chances.'

Baines ejected a stream of tobacco juice. 'It's your ship,' he said briefly, picked up the speaking-trumpet and began to bellow orders at the seamen already clawing their way aloft.

'All she will carry, Captain Baines,' said James, and went to the engine room voice pipe. 'Give us two or three minutes more,' he told it, and replaced the plug without waiting for an answer.

Men, waist deep in water, hauled on the jib halliards and the sail rattled up, thrashing and booming in the wind. The after gang sweated and strained as the spanker slowly jerked aloft, while the cook and stewards tailed on to the massive sheet blocks, dragging the boom across until the wind filled the sail to push the stern around as the head began to pay off.

Up aloft seamen hung on by teeth and fingernails, cursing and swearing at new unyielding canvas. Released from its gaskets the fore topsail bellied in the wind and promptly blew into shreds.

The *Anne Onedin,* turning into a beam sea, began to roll horribly. The engine chuntered and the rudder strained as she heeled to dip her yards under. The sea covered the lee deck up to the hatch coamings while the wild wind screamed out of a nightmare sky and the starboard lifeboat carried away to burst into a thousand fragments. One of the funnel stays parted with a 'twang' and the foremast navigation light danced away to disappear into the darkness like a firefly. The engine shrieked like a soul in torment, then with the helm up the ship paid off and brought wind and sea aft. Slowly, with a series of long pendulum swings, she began to right herself, the canvas bloomed, the bows sliced into the water and with ever-increasing speed she ran before the wind.

James rang the telegraph handle to FINISHED WITH ENGINES and concentrated his attention upon Ushant's white teeth gleaming against the dark huddle of the island, now no more than five miles off the starboard bow. He made a swift calculation of the forces at play: the canvas was holding, but the masts were bending under the strain of pushing a solid weight of iron through the water. The propeller would also be acting as a drag and he doubted the ship to be making more than seven knots. His inner eye triangulated distance, course and speed required to clear the island. He shook his head and glanced at Baines' impassive face. 'We are not going to clear,' he said.

The giant nodded agreement. 'We've but one lifeboat left, and it wouldn't last five minutes in that sea.'

'The second mate, four of your best hands and the passengers,' James told him. 'We'll launch at the last moment. They just might be able to pass in the lee . . .' He paused, once again calculated the set of wind and sea. 'No,' he said firmly. 'Belay that order.' He called sharply to the helmsman. 'Bring her round a point to starboard.' He rubbed his hands together and grinned at Baines. 'We'll take her in between,' he said.

'Not enough water,' said Baines. 'We are drawing twenty two feet. It'll tear the bottom out of her.'

James pointed overhead to a bone hard moon riding across a sky riven with cloud. 'Full moon. Spring tide. And with this weight of water pushing through the gap we might just manage.'

'It's worth a try,' said Baines, and went to stand beside the helmsman.

James' voice floated into an engine room strangely still and silent except for the echoing rush of the sea outside.

'We'll do our best,' said Albert and, replacing the whistle, smiled at Longbotham. 'They may require the use of the engine within the half hour. It seems Mr Onedin has a fancy for taking the ship through the Chenal du Four passage.'

Longbotham frowned. 'The what?'

'The gap between the island of Ushant and the mainland,' Albert explained. 'Do you speak French, Mr Longbotham?'

The chief engineer shook his head.

'Ah,' said Albert. 'A pity. But the opportunity to learn may come sooner than you think.' He smiled cheerfully and picked up a can of tallow. 'I'll just trot along to the tunnel and check the shaft. Make sure everything is shipshape, eh?' He gave a cheerful wave of a hand and sauntered away towards the tunnel entrance.

'Wind's shifting to the south'ard,' said Baines as James returned to the bridge from the tiny chartroom below.

'Good,' said James. 'It'll help push us through. Have you made this passage before?'

'Aye,' responded Baines. 'But in clear weather and broad daylight, and never in a steampot with a gutful of iron.'

The black mass of the island bulked straight ahead. The surf whitened the edge of the darkness and was now a constant roar in their ears. The lighthouse was a tall spear, from the tip of which revolved long sweeps of bright yellow light, alternatively throwing into high relief and then plunging into darkness, the forbidding rocky coast of Brittany to the east.

The sea, piling high to rush through the narrows in a raging torrent, brought an uncomfortable reminder to Baines of the loss of the *Pampero.* He found himself flinching at the test ahead, then he bulged his jaw and concentrated his attention wholly on the practical business of taking the ship through the channel.

'I have been looking up the sailing directions,' said James, conversationally. 'We can expect a tidal stream running at six knots. It sets in towards the land.'

'They all do,' replied Baines, grumpily. 'We'd best haul off another point.' He gestured towards the lighthouse. 'Else we'll be knocking at their door.'

The helmsman spun the wheel and the ship's head paid off to point at a necklace of small islands and half-submerged rocks strung between the mainland and Ushant. A fury of water raced through the narrow neck to burst in explosions of spume, whirled away by a manic wind to hang in curtains of spray that blurred the vision and masked the open channels between the sprawl of islets.

James and Baines had time to spare each other a look of common understanding before the wind's wild shriek rose to a banshee howl and a mountainous following sea picked up the ship and thrust them into the maelstrom.

By mutual, unspoken consent they had returned to their

former roles of master and mate, James donning the mantle of command and Baines slipping easily into the familiar office of subordinate. James swung the telegraph handle to FULL AHEAD while Baines concentrated his whole attention upon the set of the sails. The engine wheezed and gasped, the two remaining blades of the screw chopped into the sea and the ship ploughed towards a cataract of water foaming between a group of rocks facing them like an inverted triangle.

Overhead the beam of light raked the coast of Brittany every ten seconds, the loom bathing the sea with a pale unearthly sheen. The ship's port sidelight glowed blood red while the starboard light threw a ghastly green arc across the tumult of tossing waves.

James stood beside the helmsman, his eyes straining the darkness, seeking the first gap, while part of his mind concentrated its attention upon an image of the chart. His lips moved soundlessly as he recited to himself instructions from the sailing directions. 'First take east channel, then west channel. First east channel, then west channel.'

A pillar of rock shrouded with spray rose from the sea like a white arm. 'Hard astarboard,' he ordered. 'Bring her round, Mr Baines.'

The helmsman spun the wheel, the steering chains clattered along the deck and far aft Albert's patent steering engine hissed and chattered as the huge cogs engaged to turn the massive rudder. The spanker boomed across, the jib flapped and roared, the head came round and the lopsided screw chopped into the water to push the ship forward. The storm-swept pinnacle glowed red and slid past in a welter of foam.

The *Anne Onedin* no longer pitched and rolled but had developed an erratic rhythm, leaping and juddering as though determined to spring every bolt in her plates and break into pieces. The wave troughs grew steeper and sharper as sea piled upon sea. She bucked and yawed and the compass card spun wildly as the tide race tried to turn her beam on.

Ahead lay the Chevaux-de-Frise. A flat table of rock riven with fissures and terminating in a long row of outlying spurs like the jagged edges of serrated teeth.

Leonora woke from a drugged sleep to a confusion of noise and a chaos of disorder. Her mouth still retained the sticky taste of laudanum and her head rang like a hollow bell. She felt a rising nausea and it took long moments to adjust herself to her surroundings, so much so that for a time it seemed to be a continuation of her dream. She had been flying through the air within a vast domed glass building which she had vaguely recognized as the Crystal Palace. She had had wings of swansdown and, though totally unclothed, had felt not the slightest hint of embarrassment as she had soared above the upturned faces below. There had been the Queen, and dear Prince Albert, and a host of notables, and Mr Onedin and Captain Baines, and her father. Only he had shown disapproval, calling on her to come down instantly, while the others – and most of all, Mr Onedin – applauded her feat. She had spread her wings and swooped and glided until her father had called in a voice of thunder and the glass dome had shattered and a great wind had swept through the building bowling her over and over and stripping the feathers from her beautiful wings. She had tried to scream as she plummeted down, but nobody paid any attention even as the floor opened to swallow her in an enormous chasm. . . .

She sat up dizzily. Every bone in her body seemed to ache and she had difficulty in focusing her eyes. The pair of oil lamps burned low and swung in slow lazy arcs on their gimbals, setting eerie shadows wavering across the white-painted bulkheads. She swung her legs over the bunkboard and stared in dismay at a litter of boxes and hampers scattered about the floor. A trunk and a couple of suitcases had burst open and strewn their contents about the room as though they had been rifled by a mad thief. The trunk suddenly closed its jaws with a snap and slithered towards, her like some strange dome-backed prehistoric monster, then the ship lurched and tumbled her to her knees upon a floor which rose to meet her. She flung out a supporting hand only to quickly withdraw it with a shudder of fright as it came into contact with something matted and sticky, clammy to the touch. The lamps swung jerkily as the sea pounded the shipside, and for a moment the wicks flared brilliantly to bring her father's features into stark relief.

He lay amid a debris of hat-boxes, an overturned chair and shattered fragments of the water flask. A trickle of blood from a wide gash on his forehead had stained his side-whiskers bright scarlet. His breath came in a series of harsh whistling gasps and his arms were stretched out as though in supplication.

She crawled towards him, seized him by the shoulders and, panic-stricken, tried to shake him awake. His head merely lolled from side to side like the head of a broken doll while his breath changed from a throaty whistle to a deeper gurgling as a stream of blood issued from his mouth.

Leonora released her grip and put her hands over her face to stifle a scream which seemed to rise from some deep inner well of her being and wail soundlessly through her head. She came to her feet, and treading unheeding on shards of broken glass, ran for the door. It opened upon an enclosed alleyway echoing with the boom of the wind and the wild surge of the sea. She stumbled to the Hendricks' stateroom and beat hysterically upon the door until her hands were bruised. Receiving no reply she turned the handle and stepped across the threshold.

The Hendricks were sound asleep, snoring in their bunks, oblivious to the raging night, and hopelessly unreceptive to her vigorous shaking. Nor was the reason far to seek. An empty brandy bottle rolling about the floor told its own story. She whimpered her distress then, setting her jaw in stubborn lines, returned to the corridor in search of help.

The ship seemed deserted, peopled only by the shout of the wind and the animal snarl of the sea. She staggered along the crazily tilting alleyway, calling at the top of her voice and followed by the ghostly prints of a bloody-footed doppelgänger.

James gripped the bridge rail and squinted through the flying murk in an effort to catch a glimpse of the wreathes of foam which would first herald the presence of the Chevaux-de-Frise. The lighthouse had added its bellow to the uproar and its beam still circled like some giant cyclopean eye. He closed his eyes against the flare of yellow light and when he opened them again he saw a faint white streak pencilled against the inky blackness.

He pointed. 'Fine on the starboard bow.'

Baines nodded as he, too, picked up the tell-tale line of surf, and waved his arms in a signal to the mate standing amid a swirl of water on the foredeck. The mate was thick-set and bald with a head like polished teak. He half-disappeared beneath a flurry of the sea, then arose spluttering to raise a hand in acknowledgment.

The moon burst through a torn curtain of cloud in an explosion of light that painted the sea silver and bathed the black fangs of rock a pale shimmering green.

'Bring her round,' said James, and put the helm over. As the helmsman spun the spokes James heard a high piping call, an inarticulate plea for help. Turning his head he saw a strange apparition swaying at the head of the bridge ladder. It wore a flapping blood-stained nightdress and a mass of red-gold hair that streamed wildly in the wind.

She lurched towards him and he caught her as she fell. She opened her eyes as he scooped her into his arms. 'Papa,' she whimpered. 'He's injured and there is no one . . .'

Leonora then concluded that this was an excellent time to swoon. The arms were strong and comforting, she had performed her filial duty and was surely now entitled to the rewards of virtue. So she closed her eyes, let her head hang back, sighed blissfully and abandoned herself to the luxury of female helplessness as portrayed in the works of Mr Dickens.

James looked around exasperated, caught Baines' eye and grimaced. 'Take command,' he told him. 'I'll take her below.'

'Aye, aye,' said Baines and concentrated his full attention upon the reef ahead.

With the telegraph handle now set at STOP in order to conserve the power of the propellor for emergency use, and with the wind coming over the quarter, the *Anne Onedin* had too much leeway. She would never clear the outermost rocks. Baines waited until the last possible moment, slammed the telegraph handle to FULL AHEAD, put the helm hard astarboard, kicked the stern around and brought the wind on to the opposite quarter.

The ship heeled, rolled almost on to her beam ends as sea and wind combined to push the enormous bulk away from the half-submerged spine of knife-edged rocks, while the sheer deadweight of cargo strove to drag her back. Baines held his breath as the pounding of the engine matched the pounding of the surf and the sea boiled like a cauldron between ship and disaster. Hanging over the wing of the bridge he stared down at a barnacle-encrusted block of black obsidian flowing past in a tangle of seaweed. He expelled his breath in a grin of triumph as the stern swept clear and the rock seemed to heave itself from the water in a last effort to spit them on an outflung arm.

Baines was making his way to the telegraph handle when the churning propeller chopped into the thick mass of seaweed streaming beneath the surface.

James had dumped Leonora somewhat unceremoniously upon her bunk and turned his attention to the stertorously-breathing figure sprawled upon the deck. The man was still unconscious but a quick examination revealed that the blood oozing from the mouth came from no more than a bitten tongue and lacerated cheek. The welt on his forehead was rapidly drying to a scaly encrustation. Feeling gently behind the head James discovered a duck's-egg lump and concluded that aside from a sore head and addled brains Biddulph was none the worse for wear. He hoisted him to his shoulder and carried him through to the adjoining stateroom without so much as a glance towards Miss Biddulph's romantically heaving bosom.

Biddulph opened glazed eyes and tried to focus on a row of blurred Onedins.

'Roll over, keep your head down, and spit it out,' said James curtly, and then tensed as the ship shook to a shuddering crash that seemed to jar it to its very vitals.

'My God,' said James. 'We've struck!' and took off for the bridge at a run.

While James was engaged in carrying the supine Leonora to her stateroom, Albert was halfway along the tunnel shaft checking the over-heating bearings, his engineer's brain coolly calculating stresses and strains.

He felt, rather than heard, the impact of the blade chewing into the soft mass of weed. Slippery and slimey and as tough as rope it wound itself around the propeller boss. Under normal circumstances, with four massive blades whirling in unison, it would have been chopped into chaff, but with both blades already unbalanced and weakened it was enough to deliver the coup-de-grace. One blade fell off as though weary of its task, the other, left to turn alone, quickly followed suit.

The torque on the shaft increased. It wobbled, a long split appeared and then, before Albert's horrified eyes, it began to peel, shredding off long spirals of hot metal until beating like a gigantic egg whisk, it suddenly snapped in the middle.

Albert started to run. He felt a searing pain across his back as a whiplash length of stripped iron whirled across the tunnel to flay his shoulders open to the bone. Turning he saw the shaft bend and split to rear its divided ends high in the air. One threw out a burst of sparks and tore a ragged hole in the tunnel casing, the other speared its way through the starboard side and plunged deep into the hold.

It was the iron ore which saved them. Any other cargo and the wildly rotating shaft would have driven itself straight through the ship's bottom. As it was it embedded itself in the mass of conglomerate, glowed red with the action of friction, and welded itself firmly into the body of the cargo.

Albert felt a stunning blow to the side of his chest as the tail end tore loose and smashed its way across the narrow confines of the tunnel. His left arm felt dead, and he looked in dazed surprise at a length of shattered bone protruding through his sleeve. Then he stumbled towards the engine room, the sea gushing behind him, to be caught in the arms of Morgan who was already preparing to slam shut the watertight door.

Albert grinned at him through a white, pain-drawn face. 'Steel,' he said. 'That is the answer. We'll forge the next shaft of steel.' Then he slumped to the iron grating and slipped away to a velvet darkness with the smell of oil in his nostrils and the whisper of escaping steam in his ears.

James reached the bridge to find Baines with his ear to the engine room voice pipe. 'It's nothing,' said Baines. 'Only the engine. Something seems to have broke, so we're to proceed under sail alone.' He replaced the whistle and straightened up with the self-satisfied look of a man whose most pessimistic prognostications had been vindicated. 'Engines,' he spat. 'Who needs engines?'

James looked back to the foaming reefs of the Chevaux-de-Frise falling astern. Ushant light was continuing to bellow its warning to the world at large and its lamp carved the air into segments of light off the quarter. Far away, on the starboard bow, the Oven light winked and blinked and pointed the way to the open sea.

The sea still raged and battered at the ship, and the wind still screamed shrilly out of the darkness, but they were through the gap and safe.

'Engines can help a mite,' Baines admitted grudgingly. 'But if it weren't for the power of sail we'd have been lost. Lord, but I thought my time had come. We cleared them shoals by no more than a cough and spit.'

James only half-listened as a fugitive memory stole into his consciousness. . . .

Staggering below with his burden, balancing against the pitch and roll of the ship, he had suddenly become aware of the scalding touch of female flesh through the thin nightgown. Young and supple its message had been unmistakable and, when stumbling at the foot of the stairway, a soft globular pressure had moulded itself against his hand, he had experienced a disagreeable sense of disquietude quite foreign to his nature. All his life he had eschewed the company of women. All, with but one exception, were as unpredictable as the wind, wayward, selfish and as temperamental as racehorses. He was invariably baffled at the activities of otherwise sane men who performed prodigies of foolishness for a smile from some simpering madcap with the brain of a hen. Such emotions were but winds which forever encircled the poles of his mind leaving a still, calm centre in which a man could take time to think clearly and exercise judgment . . .

He came out of his reverie as the first splatters of rain stung his face.

'Rain,' said Baines. 'That'll flatten the sea.' He rubbed his big hands cheerfully. 'And the wind's backing. I said it would.'

'Aye,' James agreed. 'And with luck it will blow us home.'

And with luck, he thought, brightening at the prospect, he'd never set eyes on that confounded disturbing creature again.

CHAPTER FOUR

Callon travelled to the hereafter First Class while the living followed in order of precedence. First came the hearse, attended by six mutes, and drawn by four coal-black horses with nodding plumes and muffled hooves. Then came Emma and Daniel sitting stiffly upright in the leading coach, Emma invisible beneath a heavy veil and swathes of mourning and Daniel choking from a too-tight collar. They were followed by a creaking assortment of relatives each with but a tenuous hold upon mortality, then close personal friends, fellow-shipowners and other luminaries, Callon's chief assistant shepherding a scraping of clerks, and finally, bringing up the rear, a straggle of self-conscious tradesmen in carriages of more lowly appearance as befitted their station in life.

Lowered window blinds marked the passage of the cortège as it wound its way along Princes Road, crossed Parliament Street with its rows of terraced houses facing green fields, and turned into Hope Street to encircle the waiting cemetery with its clusters of winged angels sparkling in white marble. They passed the alms house, the workhouse, and the lunatic asylum, to draw up outside the open wrought-iron gates where the Reverend Mr Samuels awaited, head bowed and soul agog with the excitement of officiating at the obsequies of so illustrious a citizen.

The bearers shouldered the coffin, Mr Samuels cast a jubilant eye at the size and status of his congregation then led the way intoning: 'I am the resurrection and the life . . .'

Behind the concealment of her veil Elizabeth yawned her way through the service and Mr Samuels' interminable dissertation on the noble virtues of thrift and industry as exemplified by that staunch pillar of rectitude, George Oswald

Callon. Occasionally she stole a glance towards the stolid figure of Daniel and the shapeless bundle that was Emma, buried in veiling and snuffling melodiously into her handkerchief. Once or twice she intercepted a return glance from Daniel who rolled his eyes in some mysterious signal she was at a loss to understand. Then Mr Samuels' peroration droned to a close and she took her place in the file of mourners trailing behind the casket.

It being recognized that the female temperament being of a delicate nature was liable to disturb the solemnity of the occasion by outbursts of sobbing and fits of fainting, it was understood that they would be better able to comport themselves if permitted to stand at a respectable distance from the grave.

Mr Samuels' voice fluted, 'Ashes to ashes, dust to dust,' to a sky ridged with slate-grey clouds drifting in from the south. Handfuls of honest non-conformist earth were cast upon the mahogany-encased remains. 'Blessed are the dead which die in the Lord, for they rest from their labours,' pronounced Mr Samuels hurriedly as the first splatters of rain began to fall and a gust of wind, whimpering through the monuments, raised spirals of red dust from the raw earth.

The mourners broke up and scattered for their waiting carriages as a pale flash of lightning mottled the sky and a distant rumble of thunder heralded the end of the long hot spell. The grave-diggers began hurriedly to shovel back the earth, and a torn sheet of newspaper whirled through the air to plaster itself against a granite headstone and leave the unheeding dead to decipher its message:

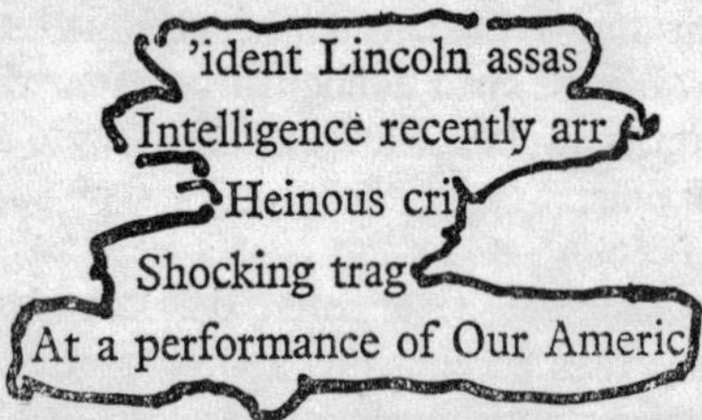

Relatives and those with a claim to close acquaintanceship made their way severally to the Callon mansion to be greeted by a sepulchral Mrs Crowther, and invited to port or brown sherry and cuts of ham or beef by solemn-faced servants.

The ladies, at last freed from the encumbrance of their veils, ate heartily and chattered like magpies while a few of the gentlemen, requiring the solace of tobacco, drifted towards the smoking-room to dispense eulogies and reminiscences beneath the incense of cigar smoke and fortified by old brandy.

At intervals tradesmen and lesser lights called to leave their cards on the silver salver standing by the open doorway, while winding sheets of rain streamed from a leaden sky and lightning flared and sparked across a deepening darkness.

Elizabeth, sipping sherry and half-listening to the burble of conversation eddying about the room, watched Daniel staging his way towards her, pausing at a group here, a group there, in an exchange of civilities. Eventually he reached her side and accepted her outstretched gloved hand.

'Thank you for coming, Mrs Frazer,' he pronounced with grave formality then, leaning close, whispered urgently. 'Elizabeth, I must speak with you.'

She stared at a face rooted in anxiety. 'Now?'

'Privately.'

The brown eyes pleaded their cause, but she shook her head. 'No, Daniel. It is finished.'

'It need not be. I have the solution.'

'As far as I am aware,' she said coldly, 'there is no problem.'

He struggled to keep his voice down and his face grave. 'You know perfectly well what I mean.'

She looked across at Emma, veil drawn back, pale-faced and eyes ringed with sorrow. 'The only problem is of your own making,' she stated pointedly.

His face darkened with anger. 'If you are referring to our child,' he said cruelly, 'I am prepared to accept full, and public, responsibility.'

She looked around anxiously. Heads were turning, and for a heart-sinking moment she believed that they had been overheard, then she realized that the glances were merely directed incuriously at the rain drumming against the window-panes.

'Really, Daniel!' She tried to move away but he kept pace with her.

'I shall call tomorrow.'

'No!' She could barely contain her anger at the fool. How

dare he threaten her security like this! Surely he understood that such an admission would destroy them both? Heaven alone knew what hare-brained scheme he had in mind, but he must be stopped at all costs.

'Tomorrow,' he reiterated firmly.

'You cannot possibly call alone. The servants will gossip.' And Albert will hear, she thought miserably. Those dark suspicions so carefully buried beneath the dust of time would rise again like horrific ghosts to point spectral fingers into the past.

'I shall be most discreet,' he told her, as though reading her mind. 'Thank you, Mrs Frazer,' he added, loudly enough for others to hear. 'You are very kind. I shall present my card, if I may?'

He turned and walked away, leaving her standing alone and afraid.

Daniel was as good as his word and called promptly at eleven o'clock, sent in his card, and was received in the spacious withdrawing-room.

The storm had rolled past and the morning sun winked through the swagged curtains to make dancing patterns across the Turkey carpet. Elizabeth looked cool and secure behind a starched blouse, embroidered jacket and wide crinoline. She greeted him calmly. 'How good of you to call, Mr Fogarty. You will take tea, of course?'

He fished out his watch and minutely examined its dial as though searching for flaws. 'I am afraid I can stay but a moment. Mrs Fogarty presents her compliments but regrets that an indiposition has prevented her accompanying me. She has, however, enjoined me to add to mine her grateful thanks for the tasteful floral tributes.'

He had evidently prepared his speech for the benefit of the maid, hovering by the door. He was also floundering and running out of words. Elizabeth could think of no weaker excuse for a morning call.

'Thank you, Edith,' she said to the maid. 'That will be all.'

The moment the door closed he moved towards her.

'Well, Daniel,' she demanded, keeping him at a distance. 'What is all this nonsense?'

He stopped short and then, hands clasped behind his back, began to pace the room in an effort to contain himself and give measure to his words.

'Mr Callon has left the company to me.' He looked at her triumphantly. 'I can now match Albert, pound for pound, guinea for guinea.'

Elizabeth looked at him in wonder. Did the idiot imagine she was for sale?

'I own everything, lock, stock and barrel,' he continued. 'Now we can spit in their eyes.'

'We? Have you taken leave of your senses?'

He grinned at her alarm. 'On the contrary, I have just come to them. Elizabeth – there is nothing to stop us. We can go away together. You, and the boy, and myself.'

'Go away?' She couldn't believe her ears.

'And none the wiser. No bones broken.' He grinned again. 'I have planned the whole thing. No one will suffer – oh, I daresay there will be a certain amount of brow beating. Public lamentations, and crocodile tears in private. But we shall soon be forgotten, if not entirely forgiven.'

She sat down weakly and gaped at the lunatic standing there smiling so confidently. She found her tongue at last. 'And what of Emma? She is your wife. You do owe her certain responsibilities.' And her own responsibilities to Albert, she thought, but doubted that argument would weigh with Daniel in his present mood.

'Oh, Emma,' said Daniel dismissively. 'She will be well taken care of. She will have everything except the ship.'

'The ship?' Elizabeth was beginning to feel that she was trapped in a waking nightmare, where the world hovered at the edges of dream and reality.

Daniel clasped his hands as though in prayer. 'In the eyes of God we are man and wife and the child is ours. I have wrestled and found my conscience clear. As my portion I shall take but one ship – the *Barracuda*. In Australia I shall sell it, and together we shall start a new life.'

'Australia? A new life? Us?' She stared incredulously.

'We shall raise sheep. Australian wool and mutton fetch high prices. Fortunes have been made, and are waiting to be made.

In a few short years we shall be rich. Rich beyond even your dreams, Elizabeth.'

'You seriously expect me to give up all this, and take ship to the ends of the earth, to live on a farm surrounded by hordes of smelly sheep! You must have taken leave of your senses!'

He seemed not to hear her. 'You will never need to soil your hands, Elizabeth. I promise.'

'The entire country is populated by the criminal classes!'

'Nonsense,' he said brusquely. 'Transportation has virtually come to an end. For the freight alone, much less the value of the ship, I can buy a tract of land the size of Wales.'

'Sheep.' She could have wept at his obtuse stupidity. 'Why?' she demanded. 'Why, why, why?'

He appeared surprised at the question. 'Because we love each other,' he answered simply.

'Oh, Daniel, you fool. You great romantical fool. All that is past. Over and done with. We cannot turn back the clock. We have obligations.'

'Obligations! The only obligations we owe are to each other.'

'And Emma. What of Emma?'

'I have told you. She will be well provided for.'

'And Albert?'

'That nincompoop?' He snorted derision.

'That nincompoop is my husband and I have not the slightest intention of deserting him on some fanciful whim of sailing off to a colony of ne'er-do-wells. You were never one to allow the grass grow under your feet, were you, Daniel Fogarty?'

'What?' The vehemence in her voice startled him.

Having him on the defensive she pushed home her advantage. 'Have you forgotten how, a few short years ago, I pleaded with you to take me away? As I recollect you were bound for Australia on that occasion also. Your first command, was it not?'

He coloured and shuffled his feet awkwardly. 'That isn't fair, Elizabeth. The circumstances were entirely different.'

'Of course they were.' She smiled spitefully. 'I quite understand. You were young and fired with ambition. I would have proved a dreadful encumbrance. Particularly to your marriage prospects.'

She watched the anger darken his features and waited calmly for the explosion of rage.

'That is not true!' he shouted. 'At that time I had not an inkling of Mr Callon's intentions. I doubt he was aware of them himself. I had no idea.'

'You married the creature,' Elizabeth stated coldly, coming to her feet. 'And now you can damned well live with her!' She rang for the maid. 'I bid you good day, Mr Fogarty.'

He swung on his heel, then paused at the door. 'I have quite made up my mind,' he said. 'I shall leave for Australia, with or without you. Should you change your mind the offer remains open.'

She shook her head and the door closed behind him.

She sat down again and found herself trembling from weakness, her mind a turmoil of self-doubt now that the moment had passed. In the privacy of her thoughts she was forced to admit that the scheme was a bold one and not without its attractions. She and dear Daniel together for always. Quite like Laura Pegram in *The Fate of Lady Chalmers*. Miss Pegram had been abducted by her lover and spirited away to a far distant land from whence she returned in the last chapter rolling in wealth and covered in diamonds. It was, Elizabeth thought, sentimentally, an intriguing prospect. But while she had every confidence that dear Daniel was a man destined to make his way in the world, it was so inconsiderate of him to expect her to abandon a houseful of servants and all the luxury that implied, to travel in acute discomfort to a distant continent where people walked upside-down. Really, the man was quite impossible!

She brooded unhappily over the possibilities. The prospect of the fool openly acknowledging parentage gave her goosepimples. The notion of him leaving for the Antipodes alone began to hold a distinct appeal. She had always believed that he would keep a guard on his tongue, even if only out of self-interest, but the death of that old barnacle seemed to have unhinged his reason. She pursued the train of thought: Mr Callon's journey to his Maker had long been sign-posted, so Daniel must have been well-prepared for his end. Why then throw away all he had laboured for? Daniel, although hot-tempered, was not a creature of whim. On the contrary he had always tended to be slow of decision, weighing the pros and cons carefully before giving voice to his views. Otherwise, she thought bitterly, we should have been married long ago. Resolutely she turned her mind away from a new entrancing dream of being wife to a sea captain, and concentrated upon the problem.

Emma. Only Emma could have driven dear Daniel to such lengths. Ever since her return, Emma's behaviour had been strange. Shutting herself up in that great gloomy mansion, rarely venturing out, and then only accompanied by the curious figure of a Chinee maid pad-padding at her side. Emma. That odious creature, Emma, must be at the bottom of it. Poor dear Daniel, she thought sentimentally, and managed to drip a tear. That dreadful woman must have led him a terrible dance. However, as Emma was evidently the key to the problem, it followed that Emma must be consulted. Discreetly, of course.

Elizabeth made up her mind. She would pay a formal visit. After all, it was no more than her duty to offer condolence to an unhappy sister, so recently bereaved. She would wear one of her more fashionable gowns with just a hint of mourning.

Brightening considerably at the prospect, Elizabeth rang for a copy of the *Shipping Gazette.* It would be just as well to know precisely when to expect dear Albert's return.

CHAPTER FIVE

Captain Joshua Webster paused to admire his reflection in the window of a hatter's shop. The ghostly image nodded its approval of the squat bullfrog figure in cut-away coat and handsome suit of well-pressed broadcloth, then raised a disembodied hand to set the low-crowned top hat more firmly upon the square skull.

The old man viewed the disjointed shade with a self-satisfied air. He'd do. Do very well indeed. Refitted from truck to keel and as smart as paint. And all at the expense of that sour-visaged son-in-law. It would have been Anne's doing, of course. Anne would have been at the bottom of it. Used her wiles on the rogue no doubt, for that miserly penny-pincher would not willingly part with a brass farthing unless he could twist a profit from it. He and the reflection met eye to eye, and for a moment an unpalatable truth hovered between them. Ever since Anne's death James Onedin had kept to his word. No longer did the haunting spectre of penury gibber at his shoulder, instead he had comfortable quarters and a regular guinea or two for his pocket. He could take his favourite tot of brandy-pawnee whenever he chose, drink like a gentleman with gentlemen, and dine off the best. To give the devil his due, Onedin had never stinted on his bargain – made so many years ago – even though at the time the promise must have stuck in his throat like a fish bone. Aye, the villain had gone up in the world, no doubt about it; and what was more, he seemed to be dragging everyone else up with him, including that parsimonious pinchpenny, Robert, and his bodkin-tongued wife.

He moved away and the image fractured to hop beside him like some sprightly gnome. Then he rounded the corner leaving his likeness forever imprisoned in glass.

Taking his bearings from the Huskisson monument he beat to windward against a tide of humanity pouring down a thoroughfare choked with traffic and steered a course into a quiet backwater of haberdashers, booksellers and milliners shops. He paused long enough to buy a buttonhole from a kerbside flower-seller, then bore away for his favourite haven, the Cubbyhole.

The Cubbyhole was an establishment which catered chiefly for the superior classes of servant and a few tradesmen who found it fallow ground for scattering the seeds of enterprise. But its most important recommendation in Webster's eyes was the provision of a private snug for the convenience of members of the gentler sex desirous of partaking of refreshment: with the qualification, of course, that they be of respectable character and accompanied by gentlemen of worth and standing.

He pushed open the door to a murmur of conversation which rose and fell like the surge of distant tides. The room was furnished rather like the sitting-room of a private house, with an ormolu clock guarded by a pair of china dogs on the mantelshelf above the open firegrate, and a painting of a hunting scene in a gilded frame hanging between the gas lamps. There were a few small round tables surrounded by spindle-backed chairs, a corner settle, and a longer bench in button-down leather, heavy flock wallpaper and a small semi-circular bar for the sale of wines, liqueurs, spirits and cordials; all presided over by the flint-eyed Mrs Jallop, wife to the landlord.

Widow Malloy was, as expected, in her usual corner seat, and engaged in conversation with her escort, a carbuncular man in a red wig whose gaitered legs, heavy corduroy, and unmistakable aroma of the stables proclaimed his calling. Her little old parchment face wrinkled into a smile of welcome at Webster's approach and she patted the seat beside her.

'Dear Captain Webster. Please do give us the pleasure of your company.'

He had first met her a few weeks past, when the course of one of his aimless meanderings about the town led him to St James' cemetery and, inevitably, Anne's last resting place. It was a simple grave with a marble headstone flanked by sorrowing angels and bearing the stark inscription:

Anne Onedin

b. 1828 d. 1864

+

Wife of JAMES

'A Most Remarkable Woman'

R.I.P.

+

The superscription had been at James' insistence and was, he was forced to admit, a fitting epitaph.

He had stood for a long time, leafing through the musty pages of memory, seeking reason where there was no reason. 'In the beginning was Chaos.' He began to understand the text. There was no beginning and no end, only the swirl of life between.

Turning aside, sick with loneliness, he had made his way to a marble seat set beneath the cool shade of a cypress tree. He must have dozed off for he awoke with a start to the sound of a cheerful voice asking: 'Was you asleep, then? I trust you ann't discommoded by my presence?'

She spoke with an educated accent and the fashionable diction of a bygone era, and for a moment he had imagined himself once again a young man with the ringleted Emily by his side; but the creak of old bones and the tug of sagging flesh quickly brought him back to the present.

Opening his eyes he saw a smiling face, shrivelled with age, and a pair of sharp bird eyes peering brightly beneath a poke bonnet. She looked for all the world like a little old hen, an illusion made the more real by a quick peck-pecking walk as though eternally on the look-out for scraps.

They had soon fallen into conversation, quickly discarding the desert of the present for the lusher pastures of the past. Her life seemed to have been signposted by great events: she was born on the very day that Louis XVI lost his head; had her first child on the eve of the battle of Waterloo, and was widowed the following day; married again, this time to a lieutenant in the King's Navy who died of wounds at the battle of Navarino. She had survived four husbands and the birth of nine children whose names sounded like a roll of battle honours.

He had listened enthralled, occasionally interjecting an exclamatory, 'I remember! I was there!' until his head seemed to be spinning with a bright-coloured kaleidoscope of memories. She had travelled the world and was as familiar with the capitals of Europe as her native Liverpool. 'I was born here,' she had said. 'And I shall die here.'

A protesting rumble from his stomach had reminded him of the time, and he guided her back to the gates along a path which wound its way between rows of tombstones, some blackened with age, some still raw with chips from the mason's chisel.

'I often come here,' she told him. 'I look on 'em as old friends waiting for me to join 'em.' She cackled. 'They has all eternity so I doubt they'll fret over a year or two more.'

Seated in the hackney he had asked for directions.

'I always takes me tot about now,' she had remarked, as though it were the most natural thing in the world. 'Perhaps you would obleege me with your company?'

'Your sarvent, ma'am,' he had replied, responding instantly to a locution he had forgotten these fifty years.

She gave the cabbie instructions. 'And move that shitten horse,' she had commanded. 'We has the devil's own thirst.'

He had forgotten that in his day ladies of quality had sworn like troopers and been thought none the worse for it. Today, men and women alike were a mealy-mouthed bunch of sanctimonious hypocrites. He doubted that damned son-in-law of his had ever given vent to a full-blooded oath in his life. Money-grubbing rogues all of them. Except for Elizabeth, of course. Now there was a woman with a taste for life. Always free with the decanter when he called, and a liking for embroidered tales of his youth.

He had come out of his musings as the hackney lurched to a halt in a quiet side street, and he had made his first acquaintanceship of the Cubbyhole.

Webster sipped his glass of brandy and water feeling unaccountably depressed. The tide of conversation had ebbed and flowed, eddying about the rocks of memory only to slacken off into a pool of stillness. The carbuncular man had excused himself and made his way through to the more convivial atmosphere of the saloon bar next door. Then a rubicund household steward accompanied by a prim-faced lady's maid rose like a pair of marionettes to the tinkling chimes of the clock and made their exit, followed by a stately procession of valets and giggling under-housemaids.

As the clock's last silvery 'ting' died away Widow Malloy sighed and gently touched Webster's gnarled hand.

'It is time to leave, Joshua,' she murmured with evident reluctance.

The sun, filtering through the window panes, carved diamond patterns on the walls and set dust motes dancing in the air. A fly buzzed drowsily and settled on the rim of an empty glass. Mrs Jallop leaned her elbows on the bar and gazed blankly at her reflection in the mirror opposite. Outside, a horse clomped slowly past, harness jangling, cart creaking. The clock slowly 'tocked' its way into eternity, and the world seemed to stop turning upon its axis.

He felt uncommonly tired. His head seemed to be stuffed with feathers and slowly detaching itself from his body. He blinked myopically at a table that began to run like wax and then levitate itself towards him. He fumbled for his snuff-box but only succeeded in pitching forward into a vortex of darkness.

He awoke to a sensation of floating on a sea of cotton wool. There was a pain in his chest and his head ached abominably. He fought for breath and struggled to lever open the shutters of his eyes.

A pumpkin face wavered against the light and a voice which seemed to arise from a tomb intoned: 'It is naught but a spasm of the heart, consistent with the onset of old age, and aggravated by over-indulgence in tobacco and spirituous liquors.'

The pumpkin became a half-moon floating away towards the blurred glow of the window and the voice faded to an indistinct mutter. A tall black bird fluffed its wings, cackled softly, then scuttered across to him on stilted legs. Beady eyes looked concern and the beak opened into a wide mouth. 'Rest easy and ye'll be mortal safe,' it said. 'But us'll need to know the names of your kin. They must be informed, else they'll be at their wit's end.'

Part of his brain understood what she was saying, but the other part seemed incapable of responding. Anne, he thought, Anne must be told. Then the realization came to him and he found his eyes scalding with tears.

She probably thought them to be tears of self-pity. 'There, there. Don't 'ee take on so,' she said consolingly, and the little hen-head bobbed encouragement.

He tried to focus his mind. James? No. Fortunately the fellow was away at sea. Robert? He shuddered at the thought of that sanctimonious moon face leering with false sympathy.

'Elizabeth,' he croaked. 'Mrs Elizabeth Frazer.' It took long moments to dredge the address from the sump of memory. A grand house in Abercromby Square. The number continued to evade him, but the beak widened into a smile of understanding and the head nodded quickly.

'We shall communicate with the lady. In the meantime you are to lie abed. Old bones need long rest.'

He licked his lips with a tongue that felt like a piece of old tarpaulin. 'Where am I?'

The hen cackled lewdly. 'Atween the sheets of a lady's bed. And not for the first time, I'll be bound.'

'Malloy,' he said. 'Widow Malloy. I remember.'

The bird peered at him and then hopped away towards the open window to perch on the sill and squawk at someone in the courtyard below.

He closed his eyes and, drifting off to sleep, the thought came to him that he had at last found a haven. A haven safe from the world.

Elizabeth was about to leave for her visit to Emma when the messenger called with a garbled story of Captain Webster taken with a seizure and begging her presence at his bedside.

The man stood before her, labouring for breath and exuding a distinct aroma of the stables. He had a homely friendly face cratered with the remains of ancient eruptions, and wore a moth-eaten red wig, apparently designed to hide a disfigurement of the scalp rather than enhance his appearance.

She made up her mind quickly. The story had a fine smack of mystery. An ancient old mariner demanding her presence at his death bed could mean that the poor old boy wanted to make a last bequest. Rather like the eponymous heroine of *Polly Pritchard's Quest*, in which the much put-upon Miss Pritchard was bequeathed a map of treasure-trove by a garrulous old greybeard she had once befriended. Given Captain Webster's circumstances, however, it did seem an unlikely outcome. Had that old reprobate been aware of the site of so much as a buried five shilling piece he would have been out long since with pick and shovel digging it up.

Yes, she decided, Emma could wait. It wasn't every day that one was called to hear the last words of an aged scoundrel on the way to meet his Maker.

The man waited, steaming with perspiration, and rolling his eyes in awe at his surroundings and the imperious lady who stood before him, flaunting her beauty like a banner.

'Very well,' said Elizabeth, and led the way to her waiting carriage.

The man climbed up beside the coachman and guided them to a quiet residential area, where they turned off into a cobbled courtyard surrounded by stables.

'Up here,' said the man, and ushered Elizabeth up a flight of rickety stairs clinging to the side of ivy-covered brick with arthritic wooden arms creaking protest at each step.

She entered by way of an arch that had once been a window, and found herself in a short dim corridor with a door of cheap, poorly-varnished pine. The man begged her pardon, leaned across, rapped the door with his knuckles, and pushed it open.

Elizabeth found herself blinking in the subdued light of a room which seemed to be choked with the memorabilia of history.

There were curved Indian knives in brass sheaths; painted devil masks, assagais and flintlock pistols; a silver hookah with braided pipes rising like a bed of snakes; a Russian samovar standing upon an oriental table; a hooded cobra in the act of striking, with ruby eyes and gold and silver scales; Chinese and Persian carpets; hangings of silk embroidered with golden dragons; a domed chest of hammered copper upon which, thrown carelessly, lay a white mantilla of finely woven lace; the walls were smothered in paintings, and bulge-eyed mirrors reflected with distorted gaze the contents and occupants of the room.

Sitting alone in a corner was an old crone in a lace cap and dress of shapeless black bombazine. She was crooning to herself, head bowed over a spray of tarot cards, and seemed to be as old as Methuselah. The ancient lined face looked up at Elizabeth's entrance, and a pair of sharp black sparrow-eyes probed and assessed before the lace cap bobbed like a cropped comb, and a voice like a rusty door hinge pronounced: 'You'll do. You'll do very well, my gal.'

Elizabeth shivered. The ancient beldame looked like the witch of Endor, and the thought passed through her mind that she had been misdirected to some cabalistic old biddy with the curse of Satan upon her.

The old biddy grinned and waved a taloned hand towards a curtained alcove containing a bed and a gently snoring figure beneath a mound of bedclothes.

'There's your fine captain, my gal. Sleeping like a babba. You'll not be his fancy, then?' It was not so much a question as a statement, tinged with a hint of disappointment.

Elizabeth bridled at the outrageous suggestion. 'Certainly not! I am his . . .' Her brain performed mental gymnastics. 'His niece. At one remove.'

The old harpy hee-hee-hee'd and scratched at a roving itch. 'One remove is far enough for old rake or young rake.'

'Rake? Him?' Elizabeth wasn't sure whether to be outraged, or amused at the notion.

'Aye, he's been a rare lad in his time, has your uncle.' She must have caught a look of distaste in Elizabeth's eyes for her lips peeled back in a leering grin. 'Like most of the young, you imagine that we old folks was borned old. But we wasn't, my gal. Once we was as young as you. And the world a livelier place. But your turn will come; aye, your turn will come.' She gave a manic hen cackle. 'There's nothing to it. All you has to do is keep on living, and one day you'll look like me.'

Elizabeth cringed at the thought. Never, she determined, never. Heaven forfend that she live long enough to resemble that shrunken old bag of bones.

'I was given to understand that Captain Webster's condition was a matter of grave urgency,' she stated coldly, hoping to put an end to a conversation which seemed to be in danger of getting out of hand.

The old lady looked past her shoulder. 'Thankee, Ruben,' she said dismissively, and the door snicked softly behind Elizabeth as her guide shuffled from the room. The wrinkled face softened into a smile of understanding. 'Don't worry your head about it, child. When your time comes, you'll have as great a collection of memories as mine to keep you company.' She floated a thin hand about the room, encompassing the relics of her past, then indicating a gilt chair covered in silk brocade, invited Elizabeth to sit beside her.

'We'll let him be and rest the while we has a chat.'

Elizabeth was tempted to refuse – she had come post haste to bear witness to an old man's dying testimony, not to listen to a gossipy old harridan parcelling out advice. But propelled by an imp of curiosity she moved across to Captain Webster's bedside and stared down at the recumbent figure.

Red of face and wearing a flannel nightgown he lay on his back, snoring peacefully and emanating the distinctive odour of brandy fumes. It was only too obvious, she thought irritably, that the old fool was affected by nothing other than a drunken stupor. It was really too disappointing. However, now that she was here, and had wasted an entire afternoon, she might as well take the opportunity to learn exactly how the old reprobate came to be involved with the harpy rocking sedately in the corner.

She therefore obediently seated herself upon the proffered chair and smiled encouragement at the ancient monument. 'I am sure he is in good hands,' she ventured, putting a questioning inflexion into her voice.

The clawed hands scooped up and riffled the pack of tarot cards, while the wise old eyes, examining her visitor, saw herself across the abyss of the years. Out of habit her hands were busily shuffling and reshuffling the cards; she splayed them out across the table and saw the light of interest dawn on Elizabeth's face.

'His time isn't yet come,' she pronounced. 'It is not in his cards.'

'Can you truly read the future?' Elizabeth's eyes widened expectantly.

'Of course,' nodded the sage positively. 'The future is naught but a map with all roads leading to the same destination. It is merely a question of choosing the right track. Do you not sometimes feel that you are in the hands of destiny?'

Elizabeth nodded eagerly. 'Oh, yes,' she breathed. 'I am sure of it.'

Mrs Malloy took Elizabeth's hand and peered closely at her palm as though it were about to reveal the secrets of the universe.

'You have a romantic nature and allow your heart to rule your head, but you'll enjoy a long life with many a sweet adventure, and lovers by the bushel. I also see a far-away place and a bitter parting.'

Elizabeth immediately thought of Daniel and began to blush, convinced that the crazed old loon could divine her thoughts.

'Old love, new love, which be the true love?' chanted the crone, releasing her hand and raking up the cards. She shuffled and cut before turning them up one at a time upon the table.

'Charioteer and Hanged Man, spawn of the devil's brood. High Priest and Lovers, twirl and twain. Star of Hope and Waning Moon, future and past be intertwined.'

Elizabeth, listening to this mumbo-jumbo, gazed entranced at the queer-looking pictures spread before her.

'What do they signify?' she asked.

'The torments of youth and the longings of age. Dreams. Touch your card.'

Elizabeth promptly chose a card showing a handsome young man being torn apart by two young ladies, one fair and one dark.

Mrs Malloy had not missed Elizabeth's sudden confusion and flush of embarrassment. 'Never lose your heart to an outcast, a misfit, a never-know-which way. Leave him to be pecked by the raven. There'll be trials and tribulations aplenty, but never fear, you'll suffer many a stroke afore your time comes.'

The old hen cackled obscenely, while Elizabeth bridled at the pointed allusion. The euphemism she understood only too well; it was one that was becoming increasingly popular in all stratas of society, bringing guffaws of laughter from music hall audiences and a fluttering of virtuous fans in many a respectable drawing-room. But it was quite out of place here. She began to realize that her companion was playing an elaborate game, with herself as victim.

'I don't believe you can tell fortunes,' she accused. 'I think you are a charlatan.'

By way of answer the old lady gathered up the cards and

cackled again. 'You are learning sense, my little cockatoo. No one can foretell the future, much less pictures painted on pasteboard. Superstitious rubbish. A nonsense fit only for children and cretins.'

'I am no cretin!' snapped Elizabeth.

'Fine clothes are no bar to credulity,' returned the old dame waspishly. 'If I forecast that you will live to a ripe old age, would you choose to prove me wrong?' She gave an eldritch screech of laughter that sent the hairs prickling on Elizabeth's scalp. Eyes as old as sin bored into her own and the ancient witch-face seemed to undergo a metamorphosis. Behind the dried mummified features, flesh lay hidden beneath flesh; fine bones revealed the ageless face of a young girl of tawny eyes and wide mouth; a wild and restless spirit embalmed in time.

'Your future is writ plain for all to see,' pronounced a voice that seemed to come from afar. 'You will know riches, wealth and power. Men will go to their graves cursing the day you were born, others will live to rejoice at your very existence. You were born an Onedin, and you will die an Onedin. And you will suffer a bereavement. One near and dear to you. Now do you believe me?'

Elizabeth stared. Was the woman truly a necromancer, or a fraud? The confounded creature spoke in riddles which might mean anything, or nothing. She opened her mouth to speak, but was interrupted by a complaining grumble from the bed behind her. Turning her head she saw Captain Webster laboriously levering himself upright.

He focused his eyes upon her. 'Elizabeth? What brought you here, child?'

'You sent for me,' she told him with some asperity. Surely the old fool remembered?

His short-sighted eyes were fogged with doubt. 'I did?'

Before she could reply, a shadow flitted bat-like just beyond the periphery of her vision, then the crone stood at his bedside, crooning sympathy.

'Widow Malloy,' he said, and Elizabeth realized it was the first time she had heard the creature's name. Then once again the old face seemed to undergo a transformation, becoming that of a harmless little old lady with a lace cap and the bowed crook-back of the aged. 'There, there, Joshua,' she murmured softly. ' 'Tis your niece come to comfort you. We've been entertaining each other with some sprightly conversation. Hasn't we, m'dear?'

Elizabeth nodded dumbly. The old lady was evidently as mad as a hatter and changeable as the seasons. She left the table and moved across to look down at the old man.

'How are you, Uncle?' she asked.

'Uncle?' His brow puckered as though his mind was engaged in chasing will-o'-the-wisp memories. 'Uncle? Niece? By God, so you are!' He wheezed with laughter. 'So you are, so you are, in a manner of speaking. And as trim a craft as a man could wish. You'll scud along in a fair breeze and leave those lumbering scows o' brothers of yours standing, mark my words if you don't.' He gave another bark of laughter and then erupted into a fit of coughing.

'Rest easy, rest easy,' counselled Widow Malloy, stroking his forehead with cool tapering fingers, wrinkled with age, but now lacking the claw-like appearance of a few moments ago. 'You have been taken with a slight morbidity of the constitution, nothing more, but you need rest. So lie back and take your ease, you are in good hands.'

The room had been muffled in silence, but gradually sound began to reassert itself. Through the thick warm air came the everyday noises of the creaking of carts, the jangle of harness, the clop of hooves, the harsh voices of ostlers rising like the distant cawing of crows.

Elizabeth became aware of the meanness of her surroundings and reminded of her duty.

'You must come home, Uncle,' she stated firmly. 'Where you can be cared for in comfort.'

'Home? I have no home. I'm naught but a beggar with his hand eternally held out for a crust.' He spoke with the petulance of a child wilfully obstinate and set in its ways.

'There,' said Mrs Malloy, softly. 'Don't fret so. You'll want for neither bed, nor roof over your head, as long as I have a penny in my purse and breath in my body.'

Elizabeth drew in an exasperated breath and her gaze encompassed the shabby room stuffed with junk like the storehouse of some dilapidated museum. 'He has a home. A fine home,' she told them, tartly.

'A charity home,' he grumbled. 'There's naught so chill as charity begrudged.'

Elizabeth's patience was coming to an end. 'You don't know on which side your bread is buttered. James has shown every consideration. You have excellent quarters, servants at your beck and call, the best of food, and money for your pocket. What more could you ask?'

'Servants,' mused Mrs Malloy. 'In my day servants knew their place. Mine wore livery with silver facings, and powdered wigs. I dined off the best, with dishes enough to choke a Sultan. But those days is gone. Squandered. When you are young life runs through the fingers like sand.'

Elizabeth gathered her skirts. 'I will inform James of your indisposition on his return. No doubt he will send a carriage.' She had not meant to speak so sharply, but her tongue always did have a tendency to run away with her. Moving towards the door she turned her head and tendered him a smile enriched with false sympathy. 'Is there anything you require?'

Webster still retained a taste for rappee, the fiery coarse-grained snuff of the Indies. He stretched out a hand for his snuff-box, opened the lid and inhaled a massive, eye-watering pinch. 'An ounce or two of the devil's dust, and a drop of Jamaica to keep body and soul together, and maybe a plump little chicken to keep them apart.'

He winked slowly and Elizabeth grinned. 'You wicked old reprobate.' Opening her purse she laid a couple of sovereigns upon a rickety bamboo table, returned his wink, and pushed open the door, to leave the pair cackling to one another like two ancient birds of prey picking over a choice morsel.

She crossed the courtyard to the waiting carriage with its drowsing coachman, and Nimrod arching her neck disdainfully at cobs and carthorses clopping over the cobbles. She stepped into the carriage while the gawk-eyed ostlers touched their forelocks and grinned sheepishly. Nimrod blew twin sighs of relief through silken nostrils before leaning into the harness and high-stepping out into the road.

On the return journey Elizabeth brooded over the Sibylline

prophecies of the aged weird. From her omnifarious reading she had garnered the information that knowledge of the future could be a snare and a delusion. Eleanor Parkhurst, for example, in *The Gypsy's Warning*, had seemingly been foretold of a rosy future, only to find herself ending her days in a Turkish harem. However, riches, lovers and a life of luxury was an enticing prospect. A bereavement was, perhaps, a cloud on the horizon, but people died every day and, who knows, it might be Emma?

The carriage threaded its way between omnibuses, haycarts, and a flock of bawling sheep, rounded a corner and entered the private seclusion of Abercromby Square, to the sight of an olive-green ambulance with a pair of steaming horses drawn up outside her own residence.

For a moment her heart jumped into her throat, and she imagined that the last of the prognostications must have been brought to fulfilment at the sight of Albert's pale face peering from a mound of blankets, as a stretcher was carried indoors.

She hurried to his side and the bat wings of superstition were dispelled as he opened his eyes and smiled wanly.

'Hullo,' he said. 'Welcome home.' And it was only when she swooped to kiss him that she noticed the flecks of bright red foam curling at the corners of his lips.

CHAPTER SIX

Robert was in his element. He believed he could say without fear of contradiction that the new establishment was prospering. Yes, definitely prospering.

It was a transformation, no doubt about it. The tiny chandler's, reeking of wax and oil and stuffed to bursting with a higgledy-piggledy confusion of tea and dates, biscuits and sea-boots, had disappeared like some poverty-stricken mendicant shouldered aside by an opulent neighbour.

Standing at the very centre of his little universe, Robert

could enjoy the best of both worlds, for the old shop had now become the grocery department of the new. The small-paned windows which used to blink hopefully at a disinterested world, had been replaced by large sheets of patent glass, tastefully decorated with graceful arabesques engraved in burnished gold and imperiously commanding the attention of passers-by. The old counters, scuffed and chipped, had been renewed with slabs of cool marble piled with pyramids of cheese and monticules of butter. Sides of bacon hung from the ceiling, while open trays of dried apricots, raisins and sultanas jostled for pride of place with plums, figs, and preserved ginger. And over all hung the aromatic tantalizing odour of coffee, freshly ground.

Robert's nostrils twitched as, turning his head, he looked along the vast cavern of the new extension where long mahogany counters displayed the artifacts of civilized living in all its variety. There were gloves of finest kid, boxes of cambric handkerchiefs, reels of multi-coloured ribbons, bales of cotton woven in the mills of Lancashire, sheaves of imported silks, festoons of muslins, swathes of chintzes and cretonnes. At the far end, stacks of India and Turkey carpets flanked by cylinders of Mr Walton's new linoleum, glowed in a cathedral shaft of light from curved corner windows. That same light painted across the floor a wavering pattern of black and gold reading: 'Rbt. ONEDIN'S RETAIL STORES'.

The shop was as busy as a hive of bees, with customers coming and going; some sauntering from department to department, others making their way purposefully to a particular counter, but all with money to spend; and few left without making a purchase.

From his vantage point he could hear the musical clink of coins from the cash desk, a contrapuntal harmony which confirmed his opinion that all the effort, the worry, the sleepless nights, had been worth while. Yes, decidedly worth while. He remembered the nights when he and Sarah had lain abed, huddled in each others arms, shivering with terror at the enormity of the step they had taken. He had sunk every penny of capital and extended his credit to breaking point, and each knew that should the venture fail they would surely be pitched into an abyss of poverty from which there was no returning.

There had come one black day when all seemed lost and he had been forced to turn to James for help. His brother had looked at him across the expanse of his desk with eyes as flat and cold as a winter sky, listening in silence to Robert's tremulous outpourings. He had asked not a single question, only nodding occasionally as though in agreement with an inner self.

'You cannot stop, you must go ahead,' he had said at last. 'Very well. I will back you.'

And that was all. James had returned to his papers, dismissively waving away Robert's protestations of gratitude as he would a bothersome fly. But from that moment the miracle had happened. Robert, who had come to borrow, had left empty-handed, but within twenty-four hours the bank had opened its coffers and once-angry creditors had come forward cap-in-hand to beg the favour of Mr Onedin's continued indulgence.

It was only at that point that Robert had come to understand something of the weight and power his morose brother carried in the world of commerce. He promised himself that one day he would be in the same position, when a word alone would be enough to save some worthy individual from disaster.

That, however, was a dream. In the meantime there was work to be done. He creased his face into a smile of welcome and stepped forward to greet a favoured customer, a lady of imposing demeanour accompanied by a starch-faced companion and a stolid footman in green velvet and silver knee-buckles.

'My Lady,' murmured Robert, bowing ceremoniously.

She acknowledged the courtesy with a trained patrician smile and waited for Mr Peabody, the departmental floor-walker, to answer Robert's snap of the fingers.

Mr Peabody advanced with the gait of a churchwarden, hands clasped before him, features grave with concern, and presented himself with a formal bow before conducting the dowager and her retinue to the department of her choice.

This was one of the moments that Robert savoured most. To be in command of an ordered world in which everyone knew his or her place to a precise degree. One, moreover, in which due deference was paid to his rapid ascent of the social ladder. Those engaged in trade had always tended to be treated as the outcasts of society; money-grubbers who hobnobbed with the kitchen staff could hardly expect to be received in the drawing-room. But times were changing: the rising merchant classes now had drawing-rooms of their own: and money had paved many a path from the tradesmens' entrance to the front doors of the mighty.

One day, Robert promised himself, he too, would be a welcome guest in the aloof mansions of the great. In fact, if business continued to progress at its present rate, he might conceivably own such a residence himself.

The thought, like some magic incantation, seemed to conjure Sarah out of the ground. Nor, considering the sulphurous look upon her face, would he have been surprised to find her accompanied by a wisp of smoke.

'Mr Tupman requests a word with you, Robert,' she announced, adding between her teeth, 'and so do I.'

Robert glumly followed her through the green baize door, strategically placed behind the cashier's desk, and leading via the sewing-room to their private quarters.

He spared a glance at the heads of the seamstresses bowed over their work, hands busy, needles flickering as they stitched, embroidered and beaded; making and altering; cleaning, ironing and button-making. This was Sarah's province; a large, airless room where the only sound was of the snip of scissors and the subdued twitter of female conversation.

A short right-angled turn brought them to their own accommodation and Robert's heart sank, as it always did whenever they entered the living-room. Jawbone, the parrot, perched unhappily in a cage balanced precariously upon a stack of books, opened its beak in a derisive squawk, stretched its wings and lapsed into brooding silence.

The room was a shambles. The encroaching business premises was squeezing them out of house and home. All their worldly possessions were piled in a conglomeration of untidy heaps. Chairs stood upon tables, and trays of crockery upon chairs. From the kitchen came a rancid smell of burning.

'The cook has left,' snapped Sarah. 'Refused to stay another minute. And who can blame her? No self-respecting cook could be expected to work under such conditions.' She waved her arms hopelessly before returning determinedly to what had become her constant cry: 'Not another day! Do you hear me, Robert! I refuse, absolutely, to spend one more night beneath this roof!'

'Mr Tupman ...?' asked Robert nervously. 'You said, Mr Tupman ...' His eyes roved wildly about the room as though expecting to find the self-effacing clerk concealed amid the confusion of furniture.

'We find new accommodation immediately, or I leave this house forever!' Sarah declaimed dramatically, and then burst into tears.

'There, there,' said Robert consolingly, edging towards a flight of stairs which, peeping coyly behind the door, led to James' office above.

Sarah slumped into a chair crackling with a litter of discarded newspapers. 'I cannot continue,' she wept. 'I simply cannot continue to exist in this muddle. We find a new residence, or I leave.'

'Think of the cost,' groaned Robert, counting coppers in his head.

'Damn the cost!' she exclaimed passionately. 'The shop is showing handsome profits, as well you know.'

Robert shook his head. 'Paper profit. Every penny earned is earmarked to pay off our debts. Any additional expense is quite out of the question. I'm sorry, but there it is,' he added firmly, the proximity of escape lending courage to his words.

'I don't care,' sobbed Sarah. 'No cook, no kitchenmaid, no parlourmaid. I cannot continue longer. You expect too much, Robert. Far too much. I've been a good wife. . . .'

'Yes,' said Robert, Hastily. 'We'll talk about it later. Must speak to Tupman.'

With Sarah's plaints following him up the worn stairway he made his way to James' office.

James had clung tenaciously to the old office crouched beneath the rafters. Deaf to Robert's threats and blandishments it seemed that nothing short of an eviction order would move him: a step which Robert had privately considered, but rejected at the thought of involving himself in a lawsuit with James. Besides, he told himself, he owed James a debt – of gratitude if nothing else. But the attic space would be invaluable, there was no denying it. It would make a perfect sewing-room and the space at present occupied by the seamstresses could be used to store their furniture and, with luck, put an end to Sarah's everlasting complaints.

Tupman's pen was scratching busily as Robert entered huffing from his exertions. The clerk stood up politely, ran a warning eye over the lesser lights scribbling industriously in their ledgers, and ushered Robert into the private office.

'Well?' Robert demanded. 'I trust this matter is of sufficient importance to warrant my presence?' He knew he was speaking like a pompous ass, but there was something about the clerk's almost inhuman efficiency that invariably reduced Robert to burbling ineffectiveness.

Tupman laid a sheaf of documents on the desk. 'I hesitated to inconvenience you, sir, but these contracts require the signature of an officer of the company, and in the absence of Mr James . . .' He raised his shoulders in an imperceptible shrug of apology and handed a pen to Robert.

'Quite, quite,' said Robert, seating himself at the desk. He scanned the tortuous legal prose, gathered that his signature would release the company of responsibility for 'loss, non-delivery, delay, damage or injury arising from Acts of God, the Queen's Enemies, Pirates, Robbers, Thieves, Barratry of Masters and Mariners, Restraints of Princes, Combination among Workmen, soiling of Wrappers or Packages. . . .' He gave up the struggle and scribbled his signature. James seemed to have thought of every eventuality including the end of the world, and no doubt had made provision for the hereafter as well.

He scrawled his name with a flourish and was about to replace the pen when Tupman laid the office ledger before him.

'The quarterly accounts, sir.'

'H'm,' said Robert. He slowly turned over the pages. There was no point in wasting time totting up the figures. They would always balance, even if the book-keeper was robbing the company blind. The thing to do was to check off the names in the left hand column against the invoices. It was not that he mistrusted Tupman – if James was content to leave the running of the office in his hands then it followed, as night followed day, that the man must be beyond reproach. But he felt that he must at least make an attempt to indicate to this impassive paragon of virtue standing at his shoulder that he had a modicum of understanding of the ramifications of the business. In short, that he was not a man to be trifled with.

The names, inscribed in beautiful copperplate, might just as well have been written in Arabic for all they conveyed to Robert. He turned back a page or two, then one item stood out like a sore thumb. He stared in disbelief.

'What is this?' he demanded.

Tupman leaned across the desk and followed Robert's pointing finger.

'Mr James' residence,' he said.

Robert lay abed watching Sarah brushing her hair in front of the dressing table mirror. He cleared his throat decisively, his invariable prelude to making an important pronouncement.

'I have given deep consideration to your suggestion, Sarah, and have come to the conclusion that it bears merit. Tomorrow we shall start looking for new accommodation.'

Sarah turned quickly, her sallow features aglow with a mixture of pleasure and triumph.

'Robert! I knew I could rely upon your superior judgment!'

Robert held up a silencing hand. 'Accommodation,' he continued, 'suitable to our status in society. The area I have in mind is Croxteth Road. I promise nothing,' he added hastily. 'But we shall look. Yes, we shall look.'

'Croxteth Road!' Sarah clasped her hands as though in prayer and her mouth rounded in a moue of astonished disbelief. 'Oh, Robert – Coxteth Road! But can we afford it? I mean really afford it? Those residences must be dreadfully expensive.'

Robert thought so, too; but he also thought of James busily juggling the Company's finances to suit his own ends. Very well, so be it; sauce for the goose was sauce for the gander.

'I think we may consider it an investment. A worthwhile investment,' he stated judiciously.

Sarah hurried from the dressing-table to scramble into bed beside him. 'Oh, Robert! You really are the most perfect, the most thoughtful and considerate of men!' She snuggled close. 'Elizabeth will be green. Simply green with envy!'

Robert made the most of his moment. 'We shall have a house-warming,' he promised, and went to his reward.

CHAPTER SEVEN

James sat at his desk wrapped in thought. Now that the Americans had finished killing one another, the whole of their eastern seaboard was again open to shipping; their ports swarming with British vessels hungry for cargoes. The emigrant trade was also on the increase; but this time the steamers were taking the lion's share, for a new class of emigrant was heading westward to the land of promise.

The starving hordes of earlier years had dwindled to a trickle, their place being taken by moderately well-to-do tradesmen. Artisans and mechanics who could afford the higher fares. No longer were they packed like herrings in dark and stinking holds. Aboard steamers they travelled in comfort with separate bunks and three cooked meals a day; moreover they made the crossing in fifteen days as against the sailing ship's thirty-five and arrived fit and healthy instead of tottering ashore like living skeletons.

The days of the sailing packet were drawing to a close and a new era was dawning. The much-derided steam kettles were now showing profits of up to forty per cent per annum and repaying their capital costs in three to four years.

James remained for a long time in brooding silence staring at a map of the north and south Atlantic trade routes, his mind fixed on a vision of the future. Then, coming to his decision, he rang for Tupman, ordered a cab, and set off in search of Albert.

He did not have far to seek, eventually running that lackadaisical young man to earth at the graving dock.

Albert, one arm in a sling, holding himself stiffly and walking with the aid of a silver-topped ebony stick, greeted James with his customary air of drawling politeness. But his face was pale and drawn, pinched lines of pain tightening the corners of his mouth.

James eyed him critically. 'You should be in hospital,' he commented. 'I don't want to lose you now.'

'Nonsense,' Albert replied with a hint of his old mockery. 'A hospital is no place for the sick.' He paused and cocked an eyebrow. 'Do I detect a note of self-interest in that last utterance?'

'Common interest,' said James. 'I want you to build me four more ships.'

The *Anne Onedin* lay dry-docked, shored with baulks of timber, her decks twisted with wreckage and alive with shipwrights and carpenters. Far below men laboured to withdraw the broken shaft.

Albert idly traced a pattern in the dust with the tip of his stick. 'Four ships,' he mused. 'We have learned much from the *Anne*. If we had had two engines, in tandem as it were, the loss of one propeller would have been of small account. We could have shut down one machine and saved the shaft.'

James smiled at his enthusiasm. 'And also a few broken ribs.' He paused reflectively. 'How many ships are fitted with these double engines?'

'Very few, and most of those were built for the Confederates as blockade runners.'

James grunted. 'Were they successful?'

'They were so successful that the Federal Navy was forced to lay down vessels of similar design to deal with them.'

James watched a rigger making his way along one of the *Anne Onedin*'s yards as sure-footed as a cat. 'What exactly is their main advantage?'

'Speed and manoeuvrability,' Albert replied, promptly.

'And no doubt much higher coal consumption,' commented James dryly. 'The sort of war I have in mind requires less speed and more economy.'

'You can have both,' said Albert. 'Those ships were driven by single expansion engines with cylinders more than eight feet in diameter. I envisage the employment of double, or even triple, expansion engines.' He noticed the blank look on James' face. 'Greater efficiency with a saving of at least thirty per cent consumption.' His eyes glistened with the light of fanaticism. 'You'll not regret it, James. We shall be first in the field. We'll build ships of seven thousand tons with twin screws, to steam at fifteen knots.'

'I can't afford to finance dreams,' said James. 'So I'll settle for two and a half thousand tons at twelve knots and with provision for forty or so cabin passengers.'

Albert looked aghast. 'Only two and a half thousand tons! A criminal waste of power! And passenger accommodation will simply clutter the decks. The ships I have in mind would be of bare, clean lines.'

'They can be as ugly as sin,' returned James. 'All I ask is that they show a profit.'

'You are making a grave mistake.'

'I have made many mistakes,' said James. 'But this isn't one of them. Prepare me some specifications. We'll go into detail later.'

'Twin screws,' Albert pleaded desperately. 'I insist.'

James scowled. 'He who pays the piper calls the tune.' He nodded briefly. 'But I'll think about it.'

Albert watched him walking away with his characteristic ungainly gait. Then he gave a wretched little cough and felt a thin trickle of blood oozing into his mouth as the splinter of bone worked its way ever deeper into his lung.

James returned to the office to discover a shirt-sleeved and perspiring Robert buried to the elbows in the company account books.

'Oh, here you are at last,' he grumbled irritably. 'I simply cannot make head nor tail of these figures.'

'For a modest shareholder you take much upon yourself,' said James. He looked down at his brother with a glint of amusement in his eyes.

'As an officer and director of the company, I have every right,' said Robert indignantly.

'Of course you have.' James smiled agreeably. 'What seems to be the problem?'

'I don't follow the ramifications of your dealings. You switch money from one company into another and then back again until everything is lost in a maze of figures. On the face of it there isn't one single company that shows a decent profit.' He sniffed. 'It's small wonder my dividends are so ludicrously small.'

'What do you expect for a fifteen pound investment?' asked James derisively.

'Precious little,' Robert admitted. 'Don't worry, James, it is a debt I have long since written off.'

'Then more fool you,' James told him tartly. 'That fifteen pounds represented fifteen per cent of the one hundred shares with which the original company was founded.'

Robert shrugged. 'So?'

'As I recollect, you squealed like a pig when asked to part with it.'

'Fifteen pounds was a deal of money in those days.'

'It is a deal of money these days,' James told him dryly. 'Your fifteen shares are now worth fifteen per cent of around eighty thousand pounds.'

'Eighty thou . . .?' Robert's jaw dropped in disbelief. He calculated swiftly and arrived at an incredible twelve thousand pounds. £12,000! The figure danced before his eyes. Lord, with a sum like that Sarah could have a dozen new residences! At the very least a mansion, and with money to spare. His habitual caution re-established ascendency over the initial euphoria. He would sell – yes, just one or two shares – enough to buy the house of Sarah's dreams – the rest could lie fallow to be garnered in the fullness of time. Raising his eyes he met James' sardonic gaze.

'Assets,' said James. 'Capital assets. Not income.'

'Ah, yes, assets to be sure. I quite understand. As a matter of fact the news could not have come at a more opportune moment.' He inflated his chest. 'For some time past I have been giving considerable thought to the possibility of changing our residence. Of moving to a better class of property.'

'Not at my expense, I trust?' James asked gravely.

Robert blinked. James seemed to have missed the point. 'No, no, of course not. I shall simply sell a few shares . . .' He broke off as James shook his head.

'You should familiarize yourself with our Articles of Association,' said James. 'These are founders shares and cannot be disposed of without the consent of your fellow directors.'

'You and Albert,' said Robert, disgustedly. 'Two peas out of the same pod. I suppose in that case I can whistle for my money!'

James sighed, and explained patiently. 'I have seventy shares. Albert's portion is the same as yours. The Onedin Line Shipping Company is a private company, and I intend it to remain so. It is family, Robert, family. Onedin Shipping is no more than a holding company whose sole property remains the *Charlotte Rhodes* and the warehouse. Total value no more than around a thousand pounds. The other companies are subsidiaries.'

'What it amounts to,' said Robert bitterly. 'Is that my shares aren't worth the paper they are written on.' He wagged a finger. 'It won't do, James, it won't do. I intend to have that house at all costs. I shall put it through the company's books. As you have yours.' He glared at James, piggy eyes defiant.

James raised an eyebrow. 'Indeed?'

'Otherwise,' snarled Robert, playing his trump card, 'I do not put my signature to another document!' He held up a restraining hand. 'No, James, I will not be dissuaded. This time you have tried me too far.'

'And what,' asked James mildly. 'Is the address of this proposed dwelling?'

Robert jutted his chin. 'Croxteth Road.'

'A good address,' rejected James. 'But damnable expensive.'

'The company can well afford it.'

'True.' James tugged at an ear. 'Well, it seems you have me beaten, Robert. I see no objection. It appears to be a sound enough investment and good security. Very well, go ahead and buy it. The company will foot the bills.'

'Hah!' said Robert, and made up his mind to buy the most expensive residence he could lay his eyes upon. Teach James a lesson. It is time he learned he was dealing with no fool, but a sound businessman, every wit as sharp as himself. He stood up and marched to the door. 'I bid you good day.'

James watched his brother's departing back, sighed and shook his head despairingly. 'Poor Robert,' he murmured. 'Will you never learn?'

The open carriage bowled along the broad tree-lined avenue of Prince's Boulevard where, secure and respectable behind walled gardens, the houses of the rising merchant class stood four-square to the winds of prosperity.

Robert, leaning comfortably against the leather upholstery, gnawed the head of his walking-stick and secretly enjoyed the fruits of virtue by watching Sarah out of the corner of his eye.

She was leaning forward, head turning this way and that, agape with wonder, like a child overwhelmed with gifts too splendid for the mind to encompass.

She stared entranced as they passed the Bishop's palace, its ivy-covered walls glowing in the evening sun. Then the carriage rounded the corner and turned in to Croxteth Road.

She sat bolt upright and clutched Robert's hand. Never in her life had she ventured this far, for here stood the homes of the aristocrats of commerce; forbidden territory to the hoi polloi and accessible only to bona fide tradesmen, the wheels of whose vans were shod with rubber in order that the sensitive ears of the residents might not be affronted by the sound of iron-rimmed tyres, nor the raucous cries of street-sellers. No omnibuses nor common carts were permitted to disturb the peaceful seclusion of magnificent villas buried in vast gardens and hidden from the gaze of the vulgar by high stone walls topped with broken glass. Their driveways were long and lined with elms, and each residence stood aloof, detached and indifferent to its neighbour.

Sarah clutched Robert's hand the tighter and looked at him with almost frightened eyes.

'Oh, Robert,' she gulped. 'It is far too grand. We could not possibly afford it.'

'We can,' Robert assured her, safe in the knowledge that the cost would not come from his own pocket.

Sarah turned her head again. 'It really is a most superior address,' she breathed. 'A most superior address.'

She gained a little confidence and nodded graciously to a

total stranger, who promptly doffed his hat and then stared blankly after the departing carriage.

Their conveyance swung into Greenheys Road, a tree-shaded lane leading away to twist and turn through banks of purple-flowered rhododendrons, and then entered a wide curving drive of red shale protected by a pair of high wrought-iron gates.

Sarah emitted a long-drawn Ooooh of surprise at her first sight of the house. It stood three storeys high with a façade of brick and stucco and was flanked by gardens dense with shrubbery and fragrant with the scents of honeysuckle, heartsease, and lavender. Laburnums hung with golden candles nodded green heads towards the sky, while a cast iron fountain filled concentric basins with cascades of sparkling water.

'Elizabeth will gnash her teeth with envy. She will turn green, positively green,' Sarah prophesied with relish. 'It really is a most superior address.'

As they drew up at a pillared portico sheltering the front door, a pale-faced man of stooped shoulders, nondescript suit, and wisp of sad moustache, hurried forward hugging his hat to his chest.

He introduced himself as a Mr Cragworthy, confidential clerk to Messrs Wichcombe, Skelhorn and Cooper, vendors of the house, rattled his keys and led them on a tour of inspection.

They trudged from room to room accompanied by Mr Cragworthy's reedy voice piping the virtues of high ceilings and monstrous fireplaces, while Sarah calculated for miles of curtaining and Robert groaned at the thought of covering acres of floors with oceans of carpet.

On the return journey his heart sank even further as Sarah catalogued the numbers of servants required to staff and maintain a household in keeping with their new-found social obligations.

'We shall need at the very least, at the veriest minimum, a cook, a kitchenmaid, two parlourmaids and a housemaid. Then there will be a coachman, a groom, a head gardener and under-gardener. Naturally, when we entertain, additional staff will be required – a couple of footmen, with a butler on especial occasions.'

Robert shuddered at the prospect of being served lukewarm soup by some grubby oaf in ill-fitting livery hastily dragged in for the occasion.

'No butler and no footmen,' he declared firmly, and mentally counted the cost of Sarah's minimum requirements, with a cook demanding thirty pounds a year, and a housemaid fully expecting twelve and all found. He came to the gloomy conclusion that he couldn't afford it, that he would never be able to afford it. These days servants required servants to wait upon servants, and the grander the household the greater the hierarchy in the servants' hall. He found it in his heart to envy James who never entertained, kept but a cook, a maid-of-all-work, and a nurse for little Charlotte, and cared not a whit for social obligations.

'And, of course,' Sarah continued, ominously, 'If I am to continue at the shop we shall require a housekeeper.'

A housekeeper! Good God, at least another fifty pounds a year! The damned woman must think he had a bottomless pocket!

'No paid servant could possibly compare with your genius for management, my dear,' he answered diplomatically.

The plumes of Sarah's hat nodded categorical affirmatives. 'A wife's proper domain is the household. I have long been of the opinion that my place is at hearth and home and removed from a world of commerce which my poor brain can scarcely comprehend.' She raised her nose and sniffed disdain at one of the lower orders trundling a handcart loaded with firewood, then drifted into merciful silence as her inner vision turned upon a picture of herself holding sway at a pleasant little gathering of ladies of impeccable taste and irreproachable antecedents.

Robert, thankful to escape one of Sarah's homilies in which, by some necromancy known only to woman, he invariably found himself portrayed as the villain of the piece, cleared his throat with the strangulated gargling sound characteristic of the Onedins when about to give tongue. James, under the stress of emotion, would give vent to a 'hrrrmph' as though a bone had stuck in his throat; Elizabeth would compress her lips as though stifling an unladylike vulgarity, and emit a suppressed whoop which emerged as a long-drawn 'mmmmmmm'.

Robert's version was an abbreviated snort, a frog-like croak that expanded his cheeks and blew gustily through his moustache.

'Once settled in, I think we might give a small dinner party by way of celebration. Quite small. Just one or two close acquaintances. People of quality.'

They sat in silence for a while, each coming to the unhappy conclusion that their circle of acquaintances was limited to a few near relatives, Mr Simkins the butcher, and the foul-mouthed Mr Jenkins, the hay and feed merchant with premises opposing the shop. None, by any stretch of the imagination, could be described as quality.

'We can rely upon Albert,' said Sarah finally. 'Albert is *very* well connected.'

Robert nodded doleful assent. Albert meant Elizabeth, and probably that granite-faced Mr Frazer; and protocol demanded that an invitation be extended to James and his rum-soaked old father-in-law. It seemed that he was going to be put to a deal of additional expense for the privilege of serving dinner to a family gathering. It was a depressing thought.

He sighed mournfully. 'We'll think of someone,' he said.

The problem, in fact, was well on the way to resolving itself. When they arrived home Robert sifted through the late afternoon post. One heavily embossed letter bearing the inscription: 'Robert Onedin, Esq.,' immediately attracted his attention; not so much because of the quality of the envelope but rather that someone had thought fit to bestow upon him the title of esquire, instead of the plain Mister commonly reserved for lesser tradesmen and those with no claim upon gentility.

He carefully slit open the envelope with a brass paper knife and drew out a folded sheet of expensive notepaper. He read carefully, savouring every word, and then blew a whistling blast of air through his moustache.

'Sarah!' he exclaimed excitedly. 'Come here! Listen to this!'

Sarah, carefully withdrawing a hatpin, jumped and pricked her scalp at the sound of Robert's sudden trumpet of triumph.

'Really, Robert!' she expostulated. 'I do think you might show a little consideration for feminine sensibilities. I almost jumped out of my shoes!'

'Confound it, woman!' snapped Robert. 'Can you not cease your everlasting prattle for one moment? All I ask is that you do me the courtesy of lending me your attention for the space of a few seconds, while I impart some important information!' Moustache bristling, he blew out his cheeks in an explosion of wrath.

'Yes, dearest, I am listening,' replied Sarah, compressing her lips and biding her time.

He inflated his chest and waved the letter above his head like a banner. 'I have here a communication from the secretary of the Liverpool Chamber of Commerce. By the unanimous approval of the committee I have been invited to become a member!'

Sarah took the letter, feasted her eyes upon the ornate heading, then devoured the contents syllable by syllable. 'Oh, Robert!' she breathed. 'A member of the Chamber of Commerce! It is the very pinnacle of success!'

Robert, inserting his thumbs into the armholes of his waistcoat, tapped his chest with self-congratulatory fingers. 'A singular honour,' he declared judiciously. 'A most singular honour. Naturally, I shall accept their very kind overtures.'

Sarah studied the letter again. 'It says here that you were proposed by a Mr Forshaw . . .?'

'Forshaw?' Robert reflected a moment. 'Ah – I have him. It must be none other than Forshaw, of Forshaw and Lowther. Fruit importers. An old established firm. Very high class merchandise. I must write him a note of thanks. But I wonder,' he mused thoughtfully. 'What precisely drew me to his attention?'

'You are far too modest of your attainments, Robert,' Sarah pronounced loyally. 'For it is self-evident that your qualities have not gone unremarked in high places.' She returned to scanning the letter. 'Proposed by Mr Forshaw,' she read. 'And seconded by a Mr Biddulph.'

'Biddulph?' Robert shook his head. 'I've never heard of him.'

'But it goes without saying that he has heard of you,' Sarah reasoned sagely. 'This, in fact, is a god-sent opportunity for making his acquaintance.'

'The dinner party!' exclaimed Robert, inspired.

'Exactly. The dinner party,' said Sarah, flushed with excitement. 'Oh, Robert – our new house will be such a perfect setting!' Unaccountably she burst into tears and fluttered into his arms.

'There, there,' said Robert, offering rough male comfort and looking into a future redolent of cigars and brandy. 'There, there. . . .'

CHAPTER EIGHT

Daniel Fogarty awoke to the sound of hail pattering against the window-panes. He sat up, stretched and yawned, and spared a glance for the sleeping Emma beside him. In repose she had the face of a madonna and invariably slept unmoving, still and quiet as though Death had stolen into the room and taken her by the hand.

He propped his head against the headboard and brooded unhappily. Two years of marriage and Emma was still as unattainable as the moon. He had tried so hard to arouse some semblance of passion; been kind and gentle, wheedled and cajoled, exploded in furies of anger. But all to no effect. She had remained the obedient wife, supine and submissive. As cold as a fish and as unresponsive as ice.

He slid from the bed and looked down. The silken sheets barely stirred at her breathing. Oh, God, he thought, if only it were Elizabeth! He rammed the thought into the back of his mind and tamped it down with the slag of despair. If only . . .! The lover's endless plea.

He padded through to their washroom as the hail turned to rain and a chink of pale yellow sunlight sliced through the heavy curtains like a golden knife.

Emma opened her eyes, emerging from the chrysalis of sleep like a moth fearful of the flame of day. She lay for a while drowsily listening to the sounds of the house stirring; the steady strop-strop of Daniel's razor, the clatter of fire-irons as Ellen, the parlourmaid, made up the dining-room fire. She stretched stealthily, luxuriating in the privilege of having the full width of the bed to herself. One of the things which she particularly loathed about the state of marriage was the inescapable close proximity of another person. She always tried to be first in bed and close her eyes in the simulation of sleep while she waited, nerves on edge, for Daniel to bump and clump about the room until finally plunging in beside her to toss and turn and thump his pillow as though he owed it a drubbing. They had long given up any attempt at conversation and she often found herself profoundly grateful when his hoggish snores punctuated the silence of the night. But once lost in the benison of sleep nothing, it seemed, could prevent their treacherous bodies rolling together. At such times she would waken, sick with loathing, to discover that Daniel had wrapped about her an arm as thick and hairy as a hawser. She had long learned that any overt attempt to wriggle free would simply tighten his grip and set his hand to wandering over her body like some obscene predatory spider. Then, her head filled with silent screams of revulsion, she schooled herself to remain as still and silent as a waxen figure until his clutch relaxed and sleep once again caught him in its snare. Only then would she stealthily creep to her own side of the bed to crouch in a huddle of misery while the earth wheeled through darkness into day.

She waited until he had finished dressing, bidden a curt 'Good morning', and taken himself off to breakfast alone before leaving for the office; then she rang for her morning pot of tea.

Amah answered her summons carrying a silver tray upon which stood a pot of fragrant jasmine tea, a tiny cup of eggshell porcelain, thin wafers of cinnamon toast, and a doll-like bowl of rice wine.

Emma sat up, thirstily swallowed her tea and crunched her toast while Amah's almond eyes set in a polished-walnut face watched unblinkingly. Then she tasted the rice wine. It was warm and sticky and trickled down her throat to burn with a familiar fire and send its fumes curling into her brain, clouding the pain of living and dulling the raw edges of yesterday....

Daniel arrived promptly at the office at five minutes after eight. Callon had always made a practice of arriving first to sit scowling in his inner sanctum, with the door wide open and his piggy eyes counting in the clerks like so many sheep; and woe betide the dilatory, or habitual, latecomer; he would find himself docked of half a day's wages at the end of the week together with an admonition to mend his ways or seek opportunities elsewhere.

Daniel, however, had carried into the office disciplines learned at sea, where it was the custom of the master to hold his subordinates responsible for the efficient working of the ship and reserving the ultimate authority to himself.

He therefore left the running of the office to the experienced Agnew and made a point of only putting in an appearance when the staff had settled into their daily routine.

Pushing open the door he stepped inside and allowed Agnew to fuss forward and divest him of hat and coat, while the subdued murmur of conversation died away to be replaced by the industrious scratching of pens and muttered incantations from ledger clerks totting up columns of figures.

There was certainly a more relaxed atmosphere since Callon's day, when a cathedral hush had been the rule and even a suppressed sneeze would bring a warning frown from the omnipresent Agnew. But work continued at the same steady pace and the chief clerk could be trusted to clamp down on any dissident foolish enough to take advantage of the new conditions.

Agnew scurried ahead of Daniel, opened the door to the private office and bowed him in. He indicated the letters neatly fanned upon the desk top.

'The morning post, sir. Business to the left, private correspondence to the right.'

It was Agnew's morning liturgy. He flicked an imaginary speck of dust from the polished mahogany surface, drew out Daniel's chair with the gesture of a head waiter seating a favoured client, opened a folder of invoices, spread a charterparty contract before his employer, dipped a pen in the ink and handed it to Daniel.

'This requires your immediate signature, sir.'

Daniel glanced at the contents, scrawled his signature, waited for Agnew to add his own as witness, blot the document and carry it away to his private lair ready for collection.

'The *Barracuda* is re-fitting in accordance with your instructions.' There was a sour look upon the clerk's face, making clear the unspoken opinion that such an overhaul was a needless expense. 'She will return to her loading berth a fortnight on Wednesday. Here is a copy of her manifest; and I feel it my duty to remind you that you have not yet appointed her captain.'

'I will attend to it shortly,' replied Daniel, reflecting that slipping out of the country unheeded was a more difficult operation than he had at first envisaged. 'Thank you, Agnew. I will ring if I should require you.'

Agnew bowed acknowledgment, gave the slumbering fire a minatorial poke, and finally left his employer to his own devices.

Daniel turned over the pages of the manifest. He had selected with care and invested £60,000 of the firm's money. He felt like a thief, but self-justification asserted itself; the company was his to do with as he chose; Emma would be well-provided for; worth close to a million if she decided to realize all her assets, and could hardly miss a beggarly £60,000; *and* the ship, he reminded himself.

The *Barracuda* was being re-fitted with care. A richly furnished stateroom for Elizabeth. . . . If she would fly with him. . . . His restless fingers drummed the desk top and his mind slid easily into the alluring prospect of a conjugal life together. . . . She must come with him! She must! How could she possibly decide otherwise? It was the opportunity which came only once in a lifetime, and for which each had secretly yearned all these years. Yes, she would come. He was sure of it. Her refusal must have been no more than a natural reaction to an over-hasty proposal. He could see that now. He should have painted a picture of a life of ease and luxury in a land of milk and honey. An escape from the boredom of life with that nincompoop Albert. If only he could meet her, talk to her again, he would surely persuade her. . . .

Daniel dragged his mind back to the more mundane affairs of the office and ran his eye over the contents of the cargo manifest: 'Ten hundredweight of glue,' he read. '890 deals of sawn wood. 500 barrels of cement. 25 cases of confectionery. Haberdashery £890. Millinery £75. Coloured cottons £400.

Cod oil 540 gallons. Five cases of plate glass. Flint glass £500. Umbrellas £30. 200 gallons of rum. 8,000 gallons of brandy. Hardware and cutlery £8,000.' The list seemed endless, but every article should fetch a high price in an Australia which imported virtually every necessity of life.

His gaze drifted towards his personal correspondence. One envelope immediately attracted his attention. It was addressed in purple ink in a backward-sloping hand and the heavy deckled envelope reeked of perfume.

Hastily he tore it open only to discover a pasteboard card whose gilt lettering invited Mr and Mrs Daniel Fogarty to a select dinner party to be given by Mr and Mrs Robert Onedin on the occasion of Mr R. Onedin's election to the Liverpool Chamber of Commerce. R.S.V.P. The Firs, Greenheys Road.

Daniel assimilated the information. That pompous ass, Robert, a member of the Chamber. And a smart new address. Another branch of the Onedins seemed to be going up in the world. He was about to pitch the invitation into the wastepaper basket when it occurred to him that this was bound to be a family gathering and therefore Elizabeth would be there.

Drawing a sheet of notepaper towards him he quickly scribbled an acceptance. Then he returned to his dream. It would be his last opportunity to persuade her. But if she should prove adamant in her refusal? His head ached and a vein throbbed in his temples with the pressure of thought. Daniel clenched his fists and slowly beat them upon the desk top. He would take her with him. Come hell or high water, he would take her with him.

Sarah haunted the letter box and counted the replies like a miser's hoard of gold. One from Captain Webster sent her flying to Robert in a fury of passion.

'The old fool!' she declaimed, waving the letter beneath his nose. 'He has written a note of acceptance on behalf of himself and a Mrs Malloy! The impertinence of the rogue is beyond belief! How dare he take it upon himself to invite some raddled harridan to our select dinner! I shall never be able to hold my head up again! Never!

'I see no problem,' said Robert reasonably. 'Simply write a

polite note stating that the invitation was intended for him, and him alone.'

He was comfortably settled in his favourite armchair, toasting his toes at a blazing fire, smoking a cigar and savouring a glass of medicinal whisky. He wore his new velvet smoking jacket and tasselled smoking hat and had been privately counting the provision of a smoking-room as one of the deserved rewards of their new house. It was really too bad of Sarah to interrupt his reflections with petty details of the household.

Sarah crunched the letter in her hand. 'I cannot!' she stormed. 'It is too late. The man is as obstinate as a donkey – he would probably refuse to come unaccompanied.'

Robert shrugged. 'One less mouth to feed. We owe him nothing.'

'Don't you understand?' wailed Sarah. 'Without him we shall be thirteen at table.'

'Ah,' said Robert. 'Awkward. Deuced awkward.'

'Awkward! It is impossible!' snapped his helpmeet. 'We must only hope and pray that she is not some gin-soaked hag from a low tavern.'

'I doubt it,' said Robert. 'Old Webster may be something of a rum-pot, but he also has an almighty high opinion of himself. He is forever boasting of his lordly acquaintances. I think it unlikely that he would consort with that sort of creature. Perhaps,' he added soothingly, 'she is a distant relative. I believe Captain Webster was quite well-connected in his day. I shouldn't worry, my dear. Just lay another place and trust to fortune.'

'My place-settings!' Sarah lamented. 'I have spent so much time and trouble – cards printed – now everything must be rearranged.'

Robert waved his cigar dismissively. 'All I ask is that you keep the garrulous old fool from my end of the table. Seat him in the middle, between Elizabeth and Emma. Well out of earshot – I don't want my principal guests affronted by a flood of coarse language. I'm damned if I understand why we invited him in the first place.'

'Because without him, James would not come. James is only

looking for an excuse. You know how he hates social gatherings. The man is fast becoming a recluse.'

'James will go anywhere he can smell business. Although I grant he is unlikely to find any here.' Robert put an end to the conversation by unfolding and shaking out his newspaper with the clear intimation that there were weightier matters deserving of his consideration than nugatory trifles which were more properly the province of the mistress of the house.

Sarah took the hint, sniffed disparagement, and stalked from the room to harass the cook and bully the housemaids.

Left to himself Robert removed his gaze from the newsprint and mused contentedly upon his good fortune. The new house had far exceeded his most optimistic expectations and, after a whirlwind visit by an army of decorators, was now furnished with an attention to comfort befitting a gentleman of means and substance. And what was more, with the exception of furnishing obtained at cost, the company was footing the bill.

The cigar end glowed agreement and released wreathes of incense to twirl and twine about his head. The smoking-room was, in Robert's considered opinion, and he ventured any man to deny it, the choicest and most comfortable room in the house. True, he also had a study for private cogitation, but that was a great barn of a place with towering bookcases, a massive desk, and lugubrious oil paintings chosen by Sarah depicting prophetic allegories on the mortality of man. But the smoking-room was his private sanctuary, combining seclusion with masculine comfort, and with the outstanding virtue of being a refuge from Sarah's ever-wagging tongue.

His reading chair was of the very latest design with a swivel arm paper rack on one side and a decanter stand on the other. With button-back plush and well-sprung seat it conformed admirably to the figure and promised untold hours of quiet reflection after the arduous demands of the world of commerce.

A spark of coal tumbled into the grate and a yellow tongue of flame added its own pale lustre to the harsher illumination of the gas jets hissing and popping in private globular worlds of their own. The fork-tongued jets drew multiple reflections from a circular rosewood table, an ebonized davenport writing desk, and a card table inlaid with mother-of-pearl. Light flashed from cut-glass lustres depending from a pair of Bristol Blue vases at each end of the mantelshelf and set a bright lattice pattern dancing in unison with the draught snoring up the chimney.

There were heavy armchairs upholstered in leather, designed in the gothic style, and for the use of fellow confidants with an attachment to the weed. An ornamental fire-screen shielded the immediate surroundings from the fierceness of the flames, and a multitude of gilt-framed pictures after the manner of Leighton all but concealed the crimson flock wallpaper.

All in all it was a comfortable clubbable room in which the more important topics of the day could be discussed free from the vapidity of female chatter, and where a man could take his ease with the solace of a good cigar and a glass or two of medicinal whisky.

Robert disposed of the remains of his cigar in the salivarium concealed in the footstool at his feet, emptied the last of the whisky down his throat, clasped his hands across his stomach and, the better to concentrate his attention, closed his eyes.

CHAPTER NINE

Biddulph looked down his nose with the expression of a man choking back a sneeze.

'I consider you, sir, to be an unprincipled boor,' he declared by way of introduction. 'But it seems that my daughter has quite taken to you. Naturally you will appreciate that my first consideration must be for her welfare. I assure you that no other consideration would have persuaded me to embark upon so onerous a parental duty.' He paused to gaze severely at James as though hoping to elicit a reply to this rigmarole.

James stared back blankly. Biddulph had sent in his business card and James had received him, practically treading on Tupman's heels, under the impression that the man had called to discuss one or two details of the coal contract. At length he found the use of his tongue. 'Your daughter? What on earth do your daughter's fancies have to do with me?'

'I thought I had made it perfectly plain,' responded Biddulph testily. 'You will find her headstrong and wilful, and she has acquired the habit of having her own way. For that I am afraid I must bear the blame. As a motherless, only child, she has been rather spoiled.' He made it sound as though he were about to part with a favoured horse.

James frowned in perplexity, realized that Biddulph in spite of his gritty voice and sour-apple demeanour was labouring under the stress of a strong emotion. Tiny beads of perspiration stood upon his forehead and he was gripping the head of his walking-stick with whitened fingers.

'Perhaps,' he suggested kindly, 'you would be more at ease sitting down. Allow me to offer a glass of brandy.'

Biddulph lowered his angular frame into the proffered chair. 'I am abstemious by nature and make it a rule never to touch spirituous liquors during the day. But on this occasion I think I may safely indulge.' He accepted the tot of brandy, added water, and glanced inquiringly at James. 'You are not taking a glass yourself?'

James shook his head. 'I also have an abstemious nature.'

'I am glad to hear it,' said Biddulph, swallowing half the brandy at a gulp. 'Alcohol and business do not mix.'

James returned to his own side of the desk. 'You were saying?' he prompted.

Biddulph stared into the bottom of his glass as though seeking inspiration. 'I understand that you are placing an order for four new steamships?'

James raised an eyebrow. 'You are uncommonly well informed.'

Biddulph creased his features into a mirthless grin. 'That is part and parcel of my business, sir. Ships use coal. I may add that I have examined your career with considerable interest. I am impressed, Mr Onedin. Impressed. On the other hand I do not care for your manners. But then possibly you do not care for mine.'

'I never allow sentiment to interfere with judgment,' said James, wishing the fellow would come to the point.

'At least there we are in accord.' Biddulph again inspected the contents of his glass. 'I will not hide it from you, Mr Onedin, were the decision wholly mine you would be the last man I should choose as a son-in-law. But—' His shoulders lifted in a shrug of resignation. 'There you have it.'

James' mouth dropped open. Son-in-law? He could not possibly have heard aright. Unless he was dealing with a madman. He looked more closely at Biddulph. Yes, there was a nervous tic at the side of his mouth and a wild look in his eye.

'Are you well?' he asked solicitously.

If Biddulph heard the question he ignored it. 'My daughter has left me no peace. She has quite made up her mind. First she badgered me into proposing your brother for membership of the Chamber, then as a concomitant, bullyragged me into accepting his inevitable invitation to dinner. You will also be a guest, I take it?'

James nodded dumbly, for once at a loss for words.

Biddulph sighed and wagged his head. 'The child's head is filled with plots and schemes. I do believe she takes after her dear mother. No matter. Naturally at first I was totally opposed to so outrageous a proposal, but Leonora has quite a talent for argument. She is, as you will discover, wise beyond her years. You may be sure that I reflected, sir, reflected deeply. Weighed the pros and cons. Came to the conclusion that the notion had merit. I will enumerate those considerations which finally persuaded me upon this course of action. Leonora is of marriageable age. I therefore consider it as no less than my parental duty to ensure that her husband-to-be is mature of temperament, of proven ability in the world of commerce, and stable of character. I may say that Leonora, being sensible of those obligations which inevitably fall to the lot of any heiress, concurs with this view. In many respects she is a quite level-headed young lady.'

'A trait which she has no doubt inherited from her father,' said James dryly.

The irony was lost upon Biddulph who nodded matter-of-fact agreement. 'My own preference would have been for a man of property. Someone with interests in iron, or railways. But I see no serious objection to an alliance between coal and shipping. Steamships use vast quantities of coal. Do you follow me, Mr Onedin?'

'Am I to understand that you are proposing to favour me with the hand of your daughter?' James could hardly believe his ears. The very idea of marrying anyone, much less an empty-headed chatterbox, was anathema to him. He again looked closely at Biddulph. The man was obviously perfectly serious. Mad as a hatter without doubt, but with all a madman's fixity of purpose.

Biddulph seemed to take James' silence for agreement for he twisted his mouth into the semblance of a self-satisfied smirk.

'An attractive proposition, don't you think? There's many a man would jump at the opportunity. But—' he shook his head at the folly of women. 'She seems to have determined upon you. For the life of me I cannot pretend to understand why. Perhaps because you were instrumental in saving her life? At first I thought it no more than a young girl's romantic fancy which, given time, would pass. I was wrong, for she has most assuredly developed an unswerving devotion towards you. You really are a most fortunate man, Mr Onedin. Most fortunate.'

James considered it time to put an end to the nonsense. 'Let me make it perfectly clear, Mr Biddulph, that although appreciative of the honour, I have not the slightest intention of remarrying.'

'I quite understand,' said Biddulph sympathetically. 'On the death of my own dear wife I was quite inconsolable. But, believe me, Mr Onedin, time brings its own balm. The memory will fade.'

He stood up, drained his glass, drew on his gloves, and bowed to James. 'I do not expect an immediate acceptance. Give the matter some thought.'

'The answer is no,' said James, flatly.

Biddulph clapped his hat upon his head. 'All I ask is that you remind yourself that you have all to gain and nothing to lose. Good day to you, sir.'

With the memory of Anne raw in his mind, James bleakly watched the departing back until the door closed and left him to his solitude. He sat for a long time, fingers absently tapping a forgotten rhythm upon the desk top. Then, slowly like a ghost sliding into the recesses of his mind, came a furtive memory of carrying Leonora down a flight of stairs, of warm yielding flesh, the tempting soft suppleness of a young body. He cringed from the thought, pushed it into a dark unconsciousness where it lay waiting, coiled like a serpent, while he concentrated his attention upon Biddulph's real motives in putting forward so absurd a proposition.

Sarah need not have worried about seating thirteen at the table, for a last minute acceptance from an unexpected quarter once more upset her place-settings.

While sifting through a long list of possibles, and firmly eradicating uncle Will Perkins, a staunch teetotaller of troublesome non-conformist conscience who could be relied upon to cast an aura of gloom over any social gathering, and cousin Wilberforce Onedin whose explosive whoops and coughs could be guaranteed to stop any conversation, Robert as an afterthought had suggested Cousin Richard Onedin. 'I doubt he'll come. Haven't seen him these many years. Not since he was first breeched, in fact. Had a card, you may remember, on the death of his father. Uncle Bob was a brewer, and young Richard must have inherited the business. Lives in Ormskirk. But I doubt he'll come, I doubt it very much. But no harm in asking. Can't have married, otherwise we'd have had another card.'

So the invitation had been sent off and, in the absence of a punctual reply, forgotten.

Then out of the blue came a cordial acceptance. Cousin Richard presented his compliments and, as business would be taking him to Liverpool at that time, he would be delighted to accept their kind invitation. He trusted that this late reply would in no way inconvenience them, sent his duty to Mrs Onedin and looked forward to renewing his acquaintance with cousin Robert.

Sarah had naturally flown into a passion and, just as naturally, held Robert to blame, heaped coals of fire upon his head, and hurried away to re-count the silver and check the dinner service.

The guests arrived in a trickle which rapidly became a flood. They were ushered into the drawing-room to be greeted by

Robert who performed the ceremony of introductions, offered a pre-dinner stomach-crisper to the gentlemen and sherry wine to the ladies.

Among the early arrivals was Mr Forshaw, a gaunt skeleton who would hardly pass muster in a congregation of scarecrows. A notorious miser, he wore a threadbare suit and a food-stained tie wound around a frayed starched collar. He snarled a greeting at Robert, peered at him as though he would remember such a spendthrift until his dying day, seized a glass of brandy and carried it away to a corner chair where he sat sipping, licking bloodless lips and mentally calculating the cost of every item in the room.

Forshaw was followed by Biddulph and Leonora. Leonora wore a white crinoline with a cascade of frills from which she arose like some delicate flower seeking the sunlight, and pushing forward twin buds of promise. Her father, clothed with the grave formality of an undertaker, stood rooted in the centre of the floor, tasting his brandy and swivelling his head from side to side as though awaiting the last trump. Leonora, however, immediately engaged the attention of her hostess, complimented her upon her dress – a rich puce matching Sarah's complexion – ooohed and aahed at the tasteful splendour of the furnishings, and thereby earned herself a friend and ally for life.

James sauntered in, nodded agreeably to Robert and Sarah, declined the proffered glass, and button-holed Biddulph to lead him away, deep in earnest conversation. Leonora blushed, murmured to Sarah: 'Such a striking figure of a man,' adding for Robert's especial benefit: 'A true Onedin. One can perceive a strong family resemblance. Particularly in the cast of the features.' At which Robert inflated his chest and permitted himself the observation that the Onedins had always been noted for the vigour of their bearing, while privately wondering what such a pretty little partridge could find to admire in so ungainly a lamp-post as James. Then, helping himself to a second brandy, he stepped forward to greet the next two guests.

Captain Webster, head high, jowls wobbling, guided his companion across the floor. The old man had done them proud. He wore a crimson cummerbund, an old-fashioned cut-away frock coat with brass buttons, and displayed across his chest the purple sash of an obscure foreign order. Widow Malloy, head cocked to one side, one hand resting lightly on Webster's crooked arm, wore a bodice of gold lace surmounted by a short velvet cape, while a skirt of green silk worked with gold threads fell to her feet in a series of swags and folds.

Sarah sighed with relief. This was no raddled harridan but self-evidently a lady of quality. Her eyes widened as Mrs Malloy graciously extended a hand to Robert and a square-cut emerald surrounded by black pearls winked in the light.

'Mrs Onedin,' boomed Webster, in a voice which had once sent men hurrying aloft. 'May I present Mrs Malloy?'

Sarah bared her teeth in a deferential shopkeeper's smile, and barely prevented herself from dropping a curtsey.

'Do take a glass of sherry wine, Mrs Malloy,' she begged.

Mrs Malloy helped herself to a glass from a tray held out by a hired footman with a breath like a lime kiln, held it up to the light, and nodded appreciatively. 'I do relish a glass or two of sack. Mind 'ee, in my day we usually supped from beakers bigger'n a mouse could pee into.' She nodded agreeably to an aghast Sarah, flipped open a richly decorated Chinese fan, and allowed Webster to guide her to a choice seat by the fire.

Sarah clutched Robert's arm. 'That creature! Did you hear? The occasion will be ruined! Quite ruined!'

'There, there,' said Robert hastily, and prepared to welcome a tall young man of pale face, a startling shock of red hair and a pair of thick-lensed spectacles perched at the end of a long Onedin nose.

'Cousin Richard,' said Robert, extending an arm in greeting.

'Ah,' said the young man, and launching himself forward, tripped over a rug, seized Robert's hand with the urgency of a drowning man grabbing a lifebelt, and jerked the arm up and down like a pump handle.

'Cousin Robert, to be sure, to be sure,' he babbled with the pronounced stammer of the incurably shy. 'You-you sent me an invitation. You d-do remember?' He blinked anxiously at Robert as though expecting to be shown the door at any moment.

'Of course, of course. You are to make yourself quite at

home. But first you must meet Mrs Onedin.' Robert disengaged his arm and carefully steered Cousin Richard across to Sarah.

'H-how do you do, Mrs Onedin?' Richard took Sarah's hand in a clammy grasp and waited helplessly for the next move.

'So good of you to come, and at such short notice,' said Sarah icily. 'Now you must meet your fellow guests.'

'Ah,' said Cousin Richard unhappily.

'Cousin James you know already.'

Richard's eyes rove wildly about the room, lit upon James talking to Biddulph, and was about to lurch towards them, when Robert intervened. 'James is engaged in conversation with Mr Biddulph – a pillar of our little community. Perhaps we should not interrupt. We shall all meet at dinner, eh?'

'Quite,' said Sarah. 'Cousin Elizabeth should be here presently. In the meantime—' Not wishing to leave this bumpkin to blunder about the room alone, she looked around seeking inspiration. Her eyes alighted upon Leonora, seated alone and rapt in a private reverie. 'This way, Cousin Richard. I really must introduce you to a young person with whom I am sure you must have much in common.'

Leonora came out of a dream in which James had proposed on bended knee, to meet the gaze of a pale young man whose features bore a startling resemblance to the object of her thoughts. He had removed his spectacles to disclose the same pale blue eyes separated by the same long Onedin nose surmounting the same pointed Onedin chin. But there the resemblance ended; this young man wore a flame of red hair above a face which was rapidly changing to a matching hue. Although undoubtedly of mortal clay, he looked rather like a poor replica discarded by the potter.

'Miss Biddulph,' Sarah was saying. 'May I have the pleasure of introducing Mr Richard Onedin? Richard is of the northern branch of the family.'

'How do you do, Mr Onedin?' said Leonora politely.

'Agh,' enunciated Richard, in the tone of a man being slowly strangled to death.

'Do excuse me,' purred Sarah. 'I am sure you two young people will find much to talk about.' Shedding her hostess's duty upon Leonora she hurried back to Robert.

'Why did you not warn me that the man was such a gawk?' she demanded.

Robert shrugged. 'He was always awkwardly shy as a child, but I imagined him to have grown out of it. Where have you seated him?'

'Between Miss Biddulph and that dreadful Mrs Malloy. My lovely dinner party – it will be a disaster!'

'Sssh,' said Robert. 'Here come the Fogartys.'

'Do sit down, Mr Onedin,' said Leonora, patting the seat beside her.

Richard obediently perched himself on the edge of the chair, hung his head, clasped his bony hands and thrust them between his knees.

'You are from the north,' Leonara began, conversationally. 'From the far north?'

'Ug,' said Richard, adding by way of explanation, 'Ormskirk.'

Ormskirk was all of thirteen miles from Liverpool.

Leonora tried again. 'Do you have interests in Ormskirk, Mr Onedin?'

'Ale,' said Richard.

'Hail?' queried Leonora, perplexed.

'Beer,' explained Richard, adding loquaciously. 'Have a brewery. Make the stuff. Sells very well.'

'How interesting,' said Leonora, having prised open the oyster. 'Do tell me about it. What is it made from?'

'Hops and barley,' said Richard, and lapsed once again into ruminative silence.

Daniel and Emma Fogarty, having paid their compliments to the host and hostess, had taken themselves off to perch in silent isolation against the far wall; Emma sitting upright, hands folded in her lap, and Daniel standing beside her in the attitude of one posing for a photograph, one hand resting on the back of her chair, the other crooked behind his back.

Sarah looked around in despair. Instead of the hope-for swirl of movement and buzz of conversation, the guests had separated into their own private worlds. James and Biddulph stood engaged in earnest conversation by the side of the curtained windows. Mr Forshaw sat in the remotest corner of the room, sipping his brandy and nibbling a biscuit like an old grey squirrel laying in a store against the winter. Webster and Mrs Malloy sat side by side on a sofa drawn up by the fire, and seemed contentedly lost in a dream world of their own. Leonora had abandoned her efforts at drawing conversation from an animated doorpost and, her eyes fixed upon James, had returned to her former comatose state.

'Circulate among the guests,' hissed Sarah to Robert. 'Do something. Or I shall stand in the middle of the floor and scream.'

'Another drink should put life into them,' said Robert and, taking his own advice, helped himself to another brandy.

Then, as though in answer to a prayer, the door swung open and a gale of laughter swept through the room as the Frazers arrived in a chattering group.

Even the gas jets in the overhanging chandeliers seemed to burn the brighter and the crystal pendants set to dancing a tinkling welcome. In a moment the room was transformed from a waxworks museum into a scurry of activity. James and Biddulph broke off their conversation, old Webster rose from his place by the fire, Cousin Richard detached his gaze from a close examination of his toes long enough to stand up and smile vaguely at the newcomers. Leonora brightened, excused herself to the lump of wood, and moved away to take up a strategic position between James and the advancing party. Even Mr Forshaw paused at his nibbling to inspect the intruders with a reptilian eye; and Daniel Fogarty unhinged himself from the wall to march forward in greeting, blushing like a schoolboy.

Elizabeth's laughter trilled around the room in counterpoint to old man Frazer's deeper boom, while Albert, dandyish in ruffled shirt and pearl-grey cut-away coat, was grinning from ear to ear. Even Mrs Frazer's long horse-face had distorted itself into a yellow-fanged smirk as she permitted herself a whinny of laughter.

Sarah, arms outstretched, hurried towards them, cawing with delight, while Robert rocked on his heels and extended the stomach of a well-made man.

'So good of you to come. So good of you,' gushed Sarah.

Albert shook Robert by the hand and cast a critical eye over the drawing-room. 'Done yourself proud, Robert. Very imposing. Very imposing indeed. Must have cost a pretty penny.'

'Ah,' said Robert, laying a knowing finger against his nose. 'Business. Wheels within wheels.'

James appeared at his shoulder. 'Must congratulate you, Robert. A sound investment. Worth every penny. Robert,' he explained to Albert, 'has been learning the tricks of the trade.'

'Good for him,' said Albert, mystified at this exchange. He took a brandy from a passing tray and caught sight of Leonora standing at the fringe of the chattering gathering. 'I say, isn't that the little filly we had aboard ship? The one who seemed so much in a take with you?' He grinned and winked at Robert. 'A dark horse, is our James. A rank outsider in the marriage stakes, wouldn't you say? Not a bit of it, that wee sheltie is longing to be saddled and ridden by only one Jehu, to wit, our James.'

'James! You sly dog!' Robert clapped James heartily between the shoulder blades. 'And I always thought of you as a sour-faced misogynist!' He leered towards Leonora. 'There's a tree worth the shaking. Fall like a ripe plum, I'll be bound.'

James' nose pinched in distaste. 'I suggest you address your remarks to her father. He is across the room, talking to Frazer.'

'I've met the father,' said Albert. 'I think I prefer to try my luck with the daughter.' He smiled affably and strolled away to re-introduce himself to Leonora.

'You take offence too easily, James,' Robert grumbled. 'Our remarks were meant to be taken in a spirit of jocularity. No one, least of all, Albert, is impugning the lady's reputation. Albert is a gentleman to his fingertips.' By way of changing the subject, he waved an expansive arm. 'So you believe this to be a sound investment, eh?'

'Excellent,' said James. 'I couldn't have done better myself.'

Robert glowed with self-esteem.

'Furthermore,' added James. 'I shall see to it that the company charges but a modest rent.'

'Rent?' Robert stared aghast. 'What rent?'

'No more than a reasonable return on capital,' James told him smoothly. He smiled agreeably at his brother's outraged face. 'Surely you did not imagine that you could gain something for nothing, simply by scratching your name across a sheet of paper?'

'But – but–' spluttered Robert. 'That means the property will never be mine!'

'True. But think on it,' said James consolingly. 'Should your business fail, you will have security of tenure. No fear of the bailiff's knock.'

'There is little danger of that,' snapped Robert indignantly. 'But what if one of your hare-brained schemes should fail? Answer me that.'

'Aye,' said James cheerfully. 'There's the rub.'

An end was put to further conversation as the folding doors separating the drawing-room from the dining-room were drawn back, and a catarrhal footman announced that dinner was served.

Robert, his evening blighted and appetite ruined, led the way with Sarah while the others fell in behind like a colourful raggle-taggle army. Leonora looped her arm possessively through James' arm, and Elizabeth made her entrance escorted by Albert, with Cousin Richard trailing behind like a lackey.

The guests settled into their places and soon, to Sarah's relief, the table was alive with chatter interrupted only by the steady munching of industrious jaws and, as a piquant sauce to the repast, a quite flattering flow of compliments encompassing everything from the graceful table decorations to the excellence of the dishes set before them. True, Cousin Richard dropped his soup spoon and succeeded in knocking over a glass of wine, and Mrs Malloy, mopping up gravy with a piece of bread, belched loudly and announced in a loud croak, 'Better belly burst, than good food waste,' while Mr Forshaw, seated below the salt, ate in greedy silence of everything within reach of his long arms.

Robert kept the wine circulating to such an extent that, by the end of the meal, everyone – with the exception of Mr Forshaw, looking around hungrily for biscuits and cheese, was quite merry. Elizabeth, avoiding Daniel's lap-dog eyes, kept the table entertained with a vivid description of a new play she and Albert had witnessed at the Royal Amphitheatre. A performance of 'The Romance of a Poor Young Man' in which the hero, from the noblest of motives, leapt from a tower rather than compromise the virtue of a lady in whose chamber he had been locked for the night.

'I do think, however,' commented Albert, 'that the chap might have had the kindness of first canvassing the lady's opinion before taking to wing. It is hardly a compliment to her charms to choose to hurl himself from a window rather than submit to an hour or two of her company.'

At which sally the ladies blushed and fluttered their fans, and Leonora wondered whether, given the same circumstance, James would throw himself from a window, and rather hoped not; while Daniel, eyeing Elizabeth, remarked as lightly as possible: 'If the lady were so desirous of saving her honour, surely she should have been the one to make the fatal leap?'

'Personally,' said Elizabeth a trifle tipsily. 'I would suffer any fate rather than death.' She smiled fondly and knowingly at Albert. 'Particularly one in which one takes so long a time a-dying.'

Sarah, deciding that the conversation was fast bordering on the indelicate, rose to her feet and suggested that the ladies retire and leave the gentlemen to their cigars.

Left to themselves the gentlemen relaxed, stretched their arms and helped themselves to tobacco, while the servants quickly cleared the table and produced decanters of port.

James pruned and lit his cigar, inhaled a satisfying lungful of smoke, took his turn at the decanter, then leaned across to Robert as Mr Forshaw, refusing the solace of tobacco, squirreled away at a bowl of nuts.

'Mr Biddulph and myself are looking forward to a few minutes private conversation. Does this magnificent residence boast a of a small private room?'

Robert sniffed. 'As you seemingly own the place, I can hardly refuse. This way.'

He led them through to the smoke-room, received a nod of dismissal from James by way of thanks, and returned to the enjoyment of the company of his fellows.

'Well,' said James rubbing his hands as the door closed behind Robert. 'Now to business.'

'You are agreed, then, in principle?' Biddulph held his glass of port to the light and reflectively examined its colour.

'An exchange of shares – Onedin for Biddulph Coal – is a proposal I can readily understand; and, in principle, I agree. There, the problem is but the minor one of deciding upon relative values in terms of market quotations and voting powers. What I do not, for the life of me comprehend, is your insistence upon making marriage a condition of acceptance.'

Biddulph sighed. 'You are a hard man to convince, Mr Onedin. Were it simply a matter of an exchange of share holdings I could approach any shipping company in Liverpool and receive a favourable answer. That is not the problem.' He paused and drew heavily upon his cigar. 'Let me speak plainly, for you and I are in much the same case. A man needs sons: otherwise there is no direction to his life. If, however, he is not so blessed, then his only hope for the future lies in a grandson – at least the line will continue. Do you follow me?'

James shook his head. 'Your daughter will produce children no matter whom she marries. Why me?'

'Because, Mr Onedin, I have been persuaded that you are the better choice. I envisage the prosperity of our joint interests being cemented by the strongest of all ties. Family, Mr Onedin, family.'

James sniffed. 'But not one likely to bring in a penny of extra income. It seems a singularly one-sided bargain if I am to support your daughter for the rest of her life.' He shrugged his shoulders. 'As for a son – I could marry a slut from the street to the same purpose.'

Biddulph did not seem affronted by James' sour comment. He smiled thinly. 'I think you are being wilfully obtuse, Mr Onedin. The child of such a union would not then be my grandson. It is my intention that Leonora will receive an income of £10,000 a year in her own right. That the first male child of the issue will receive the income from one pit until he is of age. And on my death you will become the outright owner of the entire colliery. Does that not strike you as a very fair offer?'

James put his fingertips together and reflected thoughtfully for a few moments. 'Not as generous as it would first appear. There are too many contingencies. Leonora may not produce a son. If she does, he may not live to attain his majority. You may die within the year, or live to a ripe old age. And in the event that matters fall as you anticipate, I should be expected to wait more than twenty years before receiving so much as a hundred-weight of coal. My ships require coal now, not at some distant point in the future.'

Biddulph picked at a shred of meat lodged between his teeth. 'You have but one steamship,' he reminded James.

'But I shall have more. I also have a contract for carrying your coal to Bilbao. What happens to that?'

'It continues,' said Biddulph. 'No matter what the outcome of our discussion. I am, however, quite prepared to listen to alternative proposals.'

James had used the ploy too often himself not to see the trap. He smiled: 'And thereby commit myself?'

Biddulph smiled in return. 'No commitment.'

'Very well,' said James. 'On that understanding, first a question. How many pits does your colliery work?'

'Three.'

'I take it they are profitable?'

'And will remain so.'

'For a man who earns his bread by the sweat of his own endeavours, you do seem in an uncommon hurry to disencumber yourself,' said James suspiciously.

'We brought nothing into this world, and it is certain we can carry nothing out,' Biddudlph quoted, sententiously.

James brooded in silence for a while. The man certainly seemed to have a bee in his bonnet on the subject of progeniture, while for his part he was forced to admit that a son would have been more to his liking than a sickly, mewling girl-child.

'I care not a wit,' he said, at length, 'as to how you dispose of your property, nor what provisions you choose to make for daughter or grandchildren. What I should require, on the day of signing the marriage contract, would be the output from one pit, in perpetuity.'

Biddulph spiralled smoke from his cigar, then nodded his head. 'I believe I could agree to that.'

'I'll think it over,' said James.

On their return they found that the gentlemen had rejoined the ladies in the drawing-room.

Robert, standing with his back to the fire, was holding forth on the iniquities of the proposed electoral reform bill. 'Every Tom, Dick and Harry will consider himself as good as his master,' he bayed. The country, in his considered opinion, and he would defy any man to say him nay, was going to the dogs.

His droning voice had reduced his listeners to a soporific silence, and the entrance of James and Biddulph came as a welcome interruption. Elizabeth, stifling a yawn, rose and rustled across the room, her circular crinoline with its specially stiffened hoops and alternating folds of magenta and royal blue swaying from side to side as she drifted towards the conservatory door. Leonora, to whom Cousin Richard seemed to have attached himself like a limpet, glanced towards her father. He rewarded her questioning look with an imperceptible shrug. Not, she concluded, a shrug of refusal, rather one indicating indecision. Very well, she had spun her web and could afford to wait.

Sarah interrupted Robert by clapping her hands for attention, and announcing that Mrs Fogarty had been persuaded to entertain them with a few short pieces from her extensive repertoire.

Emma left Daniel's side and made her way to the piano to the accompaniment of a spatter of applause from the assembly. She took her place at the keyboard and ran her fingers lightly over the keys, while Robert gallantly volunteered to stand at her shoulder and turn the music sheets.

She commenced with 'The Maid of the Mill', changed to excerpts from 'Love in a Village', and then, as Albert and Mr Frazer joined Robert, slid into the popular 'Where e'er You Walk'.

Emma was an accomplished player, and Mr Frazer had a pleasing baritone which suited Albert's tenor and Robert's quite melodious bass. She also enjoyed playing and had the gift of the born accompanist, the ability to anticipate and follow a change of key, thereby making the singers appear better than their merits perhaps deserved.

The notes hung and trembled, trickled across the room,

while the trio of voices rose to the ceiling and implored the ladies to 'Drink to me only with thine eyes' before then beseeching them to remember 'The Last Rose of Summer'.

Daniel had noticed Elizabeth's disappearance into the conservatory and, realizing that this might be his last opportunity, waited until the gathering seemed totally absorbed in the entertainment, then quietly made his way to the conservatory.

His exit had not gone entirely unremarked. Leonora, bored with the non-attentions of her incommunicative escort, had noticed Elizabeth's exit, at the moment putting it down to a like boredom; but then that tall, bearded, handsome Mr Fogarty had, ostentatiously sly, wandered out after her.

Curiosity aroused, she treated the hapless Richard to the smile of one putting down a deposit on future favours, and inquired if he would care to view the conservatory.

Richard, who could no more have refused had she asked him to swallow molten iron, unhinged himself from the chair and obediently trailed in her wake.

The conservatory had been the previous owner's pride and joy. A member of a learned horticultural society, he had introduced exotic trees and plants, dug a pinepit, created arbours of solitude surrounded by potted palms, giant ferns, and flightless birds cast in iron. Miniature waterfalls trickled into moss-banked pools, and artificial streams lapped their water about the roots of stunted tropical trees which, bent and twisted into misshapen poses, hung fronded arms above each secluded bower, while painted metal storks cocked inquisitive heads at the presumptuous intruders of their private retreat.

The conservatory ran along two sides of the house; a vast concourse of iron and glass heated by miles of steampipe which kept the atmosphere at sub-tropical temperatures even during the depths of winter.

A bright moon, floating across a velvet night, painted the massed greenery in shifting patterns of pale silver. Notes from the piano tinkled and trickled across the air, and the deep male voices hummed like giant bees swooping through Amazonian forests, as Leonora took Richard's sticky hand and guided him through a jungle of nodding ferns and whispering palms. Discovering an alcove with a rustic garden seat, she released his clammy grip, spread her crinoline, and settled herself comfortably. Attuning her eyes to the gloom, she sought for a glimpse of Elizabeth and her follower, but both seemed to have been swallowed into the outer darkness.

Richard, apparently taking her silence for reproof, coughed, wriggled uncomfortably, and mopped his brow.

'I feel you must find me poor company, Miss Biddulph,' he ventured.

Leonora stopped straining her vision and dutifully returned her attention to her escort. She sighed. 'Well, quite frankly, yes I do, Mr Onedin.'

He seemed to accept it as a fact of life. Clasping his hands he stared at his thumbs. 'I cannot help myself. I am afraid I fall into a d-dreadful state of witlessness when in the p-presence of th-the fairer sex.'

Leonora laughed lightly. 'It is far from flattering to be told that one's presence so discommodes a gentleman that his tongue positively ties itself in knots.'

Richard nodded morose agreement. 'The more delectable the creature, the worse I become.'

Leonora was touched, and not a little flattered. She took one of his hands, and patted it as though comforting a child. 'Poor Richard,' she murmured softly. 'Poor Richard.'

The conservatory was close and stickily humid. Perspiration glistened damply on Richard's face and his spectacles became opaque with condensation. He turned a blind man's gaze upon her and removed the eye-pieces to stare myopically at a petite face with a wide smiling mouth, white teeth and brown eyes alive with sympathy. His heart began to bang in his chest and unconsciously he tightened his grip of her hand like a drowning man clinging to a lifeline. He suddenly found his tongue and spoke rapidly in short staccato phrases.

'I have never known a social life you see? My father believed that one should start at the beginning. The way to success is in keeping your nose to the grindstone, he would say. He kept mine pressed firmly down until I was nineteen years of age. Then he died. He was a hard man. I never knew my mother. She died when I was born. . . .'

Leonora nodded. 'Like me.'

'... The responsibility for the continuation of the brewery became mine. I was an only child.'

'Brewery? You are a brewer?' Leonora had imagined brewers as enormous men in leather aprons.

'Brewmaster,' Richard corrected. 'Our own brewery. Good Ale. Very good. Pure. We would not tolerate adulteration. Father, a good brewer, but no head for business. Only one way. Expansion. I contracted with inns, coach houses, common ale houses to sell our ale to the exclusion of others. I believe I have made a tolerable success. Profits increased, so I ventured into other businesses. An investment here, an investment there. I am chairman of three companies and sit on the board of four others.' His voice took on a gritty quality. 'And I do assure you that I am no sleeping partner. When I speak, they listen, and it is a bold man who crosses me.'

Leonora looked at him quickly, but it was obvious that he was simply stating a fact, not boasting. It was also evident that this young man was not the incompetent idiot he appeared to be. She shook her head. 'To have so much authority, and yet be in such mortal terror of the weaker sex!'

Richard heaved a heartfelt sigh. 'I curse myself for my ineptitude, but female company invariably reduces me to a jelly. I never know what is expected of me, and I am afraid that I have never learned the art of small talk.' His eyes left her gaze, ran over her like a pair of mice in harness, then fixed themselves bashfully upon the dripping frond of a palm.

For a brief moment she had the uncanny feeling of being divested of clothing. Intuitively she straightened her back and pushed out her protuberances, while a warmth coursed through her veins and she found herself unaccountably blushing. Her throat felt strangely dry and her heart beat a quick pit-a-pat rhythm.

'Do you realize', she asked. 'That you have spoken for a full five minutes, and not stammered once?'

He seemed to consider the implications then nodded gravely. 'Unusual,' he said. 'Most unusual. You have a most sympathetic nature, Miss Biddulph.'

'Leonora,' she said.

'Miss Leonora.'

They smiled at each other as though a barrier had been surmounted. He was, she thought, a typical Onedin, not entirely unlike James in many ways. The wish was father to the thought: 'What do you know of your cousin James?' she asked.

'James? Now there is a man after my own heart. Sharp as a needle. I have followed his career with close interest. Made inquiries once. Thought to buy into one of his companies. But James keeps a stranglehold. Dividends fair, but no power to the boards. Not for me, I'm afraid. Cousin James will go far, mark my words. Always thought so. Even as a child he walked alone. . . .'

The moon scudded behind a hummock of cloud to plunge the conservatory into velvet darkness. Moisture dripped from alien plants rustling and stretching with age-old memories. The suffocating jungle-smell of decaying vegetation hung like a miasma in the steaming air. In the house the singers had paused for breath, and only the liquid notes of the piano disturbed the silence.

Leonora shivered and moved closer, and with an instinct as old as time drew his hand to her waist. He saw her face a white blur in the darkness, and then soft lips gently brushed against his mouth. His hand, with a volition of its own, moved upwards seeking to encompass a soft perfection moulding to his touch. She sighed and murmured blissfully, pushed her torso forward and on the instant James was forgotten, and her carefully laid plots and schemes swept away in the realization that Mr Richard Onedin was far and away the nicest, kindest, man one could possibly hope to meet. Experimentally she ran the tip of her tongue along his upper lip and the nice kind man quivered, and then suddenly sat bolt upright in alarm.

'My dear, Miss Biddulph!', he gasped. 'Whatever must you think of me! I have compromised you utterly!'

'In which case,' she said gravely. 'You must pay the forfeit. A gentleman could do no other.'

'Anything,' he breathed. 'Anything you command.'

'Very well. For the next two weeks you are condemned to be my escort. You are to accompany me to the opera, to the theatre, and, if you are by then sufficiently contrite, you may take me to dinner.'

'A penalty,' said Richard earnestly and without the trace of a stammer. 'Which I shall undertake with all my heart. I am not deserving of so rich a reward.'

'Well,' said Leonora judiciously. 'It is high time someone took you in hand.'

They sat contentedly side by side, hand holding hand, wrapped in secretive darkness, the only sound the faint hissing of the steam pipes. The last distant cadences of the piano had faded into silence while far over their heads the moon plunged deeper into the cloud, betraying its presence only by a surrounding aureole of ghostly light.

Footsteps crunching on gravel brought them to startled awareness. Leonora, anticipating that Richard was about to make their presence known, reached out and put a warning finger to his lips. With luck, hidden in their arbour, they would remain undiscovered. Her mind raced quickly. To jest of being compromised was one thing, but disclosure was entirely another. Her father's fury would know no bounds, and she would most certainly be forbidden to so much as set eyes on this delightful young man ever again. Her life would be blighted. She would be forced into marriage quickly with that odious James when she could conceive of no other existence except with dear, tongue-tied Richard.

Her eyes tried to pierce the darkness but all she could distinguish was the pale blur of glass against the night sky and the writhing silhouettes of tropic foliage.

Voices rose and fell, a low sibilant whispering with a chord of anger punctuating discordant phrasing. The footsteps came closer, then stopped, interrupting the muttered argument.

'Wait – sit here – for a moment,' pleaded a deep male voice.

Then the moon momentarily escaped from its prison and a web of light made lattic patterns in the darkness, picking out Elizabeth and Daniel Fogarty standing face to face, stiff with anger.

'No!'

He took Elizabeth roughly by the arm and swung her out of sight into the depths of a bower similar to their own. The disagreement continued but in tones so muted that only disjointed sentences, heated by temper, were recognizable.

Leonora brushed aside a tendril of hair and listened intently, unashamedly eavesdropping, and by distinguishing between guttural male and lighter female pitch was able to make rudimentary sense of a controversy which became more intriguing by the moment.

'Please. You must reconsider,' His voice. Low. Urgent.

'No.'

'You will not regret it. I promise.'

'No. It is over.'

A dribble of argument. Fraying tempers.

'I must see him.'

'He does not know. He must never know. Go your ways and leave us in peace.'

'I have the right.'

'No.'

Hissing expostulations. The jarring collision of avowal and disavowal. Silence, and a soft weeping.

Richard shifted uneasily, an unwilling accomplice. Leonora stayed him with a hand upon his arm and, craning forward, gently parted the frayed edges of a giant fern until she could just barely discern the outlines of the two figures.

Elizabeth was seated, head bent, face cupped in her hands. He stood, a hand on her shoulder, awkwardly offering comfort.

Evidently her tears won the day for he sighed deeply and moved back a pace.

'Very well,' he said, in the resigned tone of one accepting defeat. 'I will trouble you no further. All I ask is that you grant me one last favour.'

'What?' The moonlight picked out the pale face raised in misery.

'The *Barracuda* sails on Wednesday, by the morning tide. Will you come down to the ship? To say farewell?'

She hesitated, uncertain. 'I don't know.'

'It will be the last time. We shall never meet again.'

'I'll try.'

'And bring the boy.'

'The boy?'

'You owe me that at least.'

'I owe you nothing.'

'You can't deny me.'

Again the hesitation. 'You will not tell him?'

'Never, without your permission.'

She took time to think by dabbing her eyes with a shred of cambric. 'It may not be possible.'

'Make it possible.'

'I'll try.'

The moon once more buried its face and the world turned black.

A slight scuffling sound. 'No, Daniel! No!'

The quick tip-tap of feet, followed by a longer male tread.

Leonora and Richard huddled into deeper concealment as two shadows moved across their vision and then were gone.

They waited an unconscionable time, holding their breath, until the snick of the door catch confirmed that they were once again alone.

Richard mopped his brow. 'W-what on earth was that about?'

Leonora, glowing with excitement, clutched his arm. 'They have been having an affair of the heart!'

'Cousin Elizabeth! I don't believe it!'

'She has just broken it off. The poor man was so distraught.' She sighed sentimentally. 'Unrequited love.'

'*Cousin* Elizabeth!' Richard repeated, as though sheer repetition would exercise the evidence of his ears. Cousin *Elizabeth*!'

'The boy?' mused Leonora. 'I wonder what that meant?'

'I don't know,' said Richard. 'And I don't want to know. This,' he added firmly, 'must go no further.'

'Of course not,' agreed Leonora, longing for a confidante.

'The scandal would destroy them. Both families. My God – isn't he married to Callon's daughter? The fool! What the devil possessed the man?'

'Love knows no bounds,' murmured Leonora, squeezing his hand.

'If it doesn't,' said Richard. 'Shares will tumble. Callon has holdings in coal, iron and rail.'

'You sound just like my father!', Leonora withdrew her hand and patted her hair back into place. 'Don't you men ever think of anything but your silly old stocks and shares?'

'Those silly old stocks and shares,' said Richard stiffly. 'Pay for your bonnets and ribbons.'

Leonora snorted, stood up and smoothed her dress. 'I think it past time that we returned, Mr Onedin,' she said stiffly.

'As you w-wish, Miss B-Biddulph,' Richard replied, equally coolly, and with the sensation of a man falling over a cliff. At a loss to understand how the conversation could have taken so disastrous a turn he escorted her to the door, tripping over his feet and entangling himself with an overhanding vine, and burdened with the conviction that he would never set eyes on this delectable creature ever again.

As they entered the drawing-room, Emma's fingers rippled over the keys and the group about the piano, now augmented by James, raised their voices to the tune of 'The Minstrel Boy'. Elizabeth had joined Mr and Mrs Frazer and was sitting, calm and composed and looking as though butter would not melt in her mouth. Daniel Fogarty had taken his stance beside Emma's vacated chair, and stood scowling at the room at large.

Leonora, eyes demurely lowered, guided Richard across to their previous situation, smiled innocently at her father's suspicious glance, disposed her dress into neat folds, and concentrated her attention upon the singers.

Richard stumbled to his chair blushing hideously, loosed a hiccup like an exploding paper bag, clasped his bony hands together, entwined his ankles and wished he were dead. Women. If he lived to be a thousand, he would never understand women.

CHAPTER TEN

James was breakfasting alone when Albert marched in unannounced. He carried a roll of ship plans tucked beneath one arm, bade James a cheerful good-morning, and began to clear a space on the table.

'You are up betimes.' James poured a second cup of coffee

and eyed Albert curiously. He seemed to have made a complete recovery from his injuries, but he also had the pale withdrawn look of a man burning up his energies.

Albert took the cup of coffee, added milk and sugar, and drank gratefully.

'Haven't been to bed yet. Wanted to finish these, and canvass your opinion before sending them off to the draughtsmen.'

He spread the plans on the cleared space, weighted them down with milk jug and salt cellar, and stood back proudly.

'There isn't that much urgency,' said James. He pushed aside his unfinished breakfast and leaned over the drawings.

'General arrangement plan,' said Albert. 'Only sketched in as yet, of course, but have incorporated one or two modifications which should interest you.'

Albert's notion of sketching-in revealed itself as meticulously drawn, detailed plans of every deck, and showing the precise layout of every feature from the windlass on the forecastle head to the situation of the steering wheel on the open bridge.

'The cargo holds – two forward and one aft – each served by four derricks and four steam winches. You'll be able to off-load into lighters in any port in the world, James.' His finger darted across the plan. 'Bridge walk above the master's quarters. Enclosed chart-room with direct access to the bridge. Officers' and passengers' accommodation. Dining-saloon. Engineers live aft. Improved steering engine house above the rudder post. Right-aft, a small house for the donkey engine.'

'A what?'

'An auxiliary engine for supplying steam to feed pumps, deck winches, and so on. Very useful piece of equipment. More properly should be called a Duncan, I daresay, after the fellow who first thought of it. Poor chap, he'll probably go down in history as an ass. I say, this is very good coffee. Could I trouble you for another?'

James re-filled Albert's cup. 'And what,' he asked suspiciously. 'Are these refinements going to cost me?'

'About £50,000,' said Albert. 'This really is remarkably good coffee.'

Four ships. Two hundred thousand pounds. Not too large a sum to raise by public subscription. He turned over the top sheet. 'Very well, Albert, let us take a more detailed look at what I can expect for my money.'

The next plan showed sectional drawings of the engine room, and Albert enthusiastically babbled of coefficients of expansion, pressures per square inch, blow-down valves and reverse atmospheric valves, of twin propellers and double expansion engines, of Scotch boilers and oddly named superheaters.

James listened patiently, and then cut him short. 'Coal,' he asked, coming to the topic uppermost in his mind. 'How much coal will it burn?'

'Two pounds per horsepower per hour,' Albert replied promptly. He saw the baffled look on James' face. 'About one and three quarter tons per hour at a cruising speed of twelve knots.'

James calculated swiftly. One and three quarter tons would cost about forty two pounds per day. On a three month voyage that would represent £3,500 going up the chimney in smoke. On the other hand, he reflected, he could have the contents of a coal mine entirely free simply by accepting Biddulph's offer. It would give him an enormous advantage over his competitors. He nodded slowly to himself, then glancing up, caught a reproachful look from Anne's portrait hung above the fireplace.

Albert apparently took his nod for an affirmative. 'You agree?'

'Two engines?'

'You'll not regret it.'

'Very well, Albert. Two engines. Build me four ships to the identical pattern.'

'Identical?'

'To the last nut and bolt,' James told him decisively. 'How can I be expected to work out accurate operating costs if no two ships are alike?'

'Technology is moving apace, James. One new development spawns a dozen others. Take steel, for example. Lighter in weight and of far higher tensile strength. In the not so distant future ships will be built entirely of steel.'

'Always tomorrow, never today.'

'There are a few minor problems,' Albert admitted. 'Cost for one. £50 a ton as against £8–10 for iron. Not enough rolling mills, not enough experience. And there are occasional flaws in its manufacture, but they will be overcome.'

'Not at my expense,' said James. 'I'll wait.'

Their conversation was interrupted by the arrival of Captain Webster attired in nightcap, dressing-gown and carpet slippers. He yawned, rubbed sleep from his eyes, and steered a course for the sideboard with its array of chafing dishes. They watched him help himself to a liberal plateful of bacon and kidneys, to which he added a sausage, a couple of fried eggs and a mound of fried potatoes. He then ladled on a generous dollop of chutney and dosed the mixture with a vigorous shaking of cayenne before making his way to his usual place at the far end of the long table. He raised a forkful to his mouth, met their fascinated gaze, mumbled a perfunctory 'g'morning', and with no further heed applied himself to his victuals.

'It must be one of the consolations of old age,' Albert murmured faintly. He averted his eyes and commenced to roll up his plans. 'By the by, it is strongly rumoured that you are contemplating embarking upon the sea of matrimony once again. No truth in it, I suppose?'

'Why?' James demanded irritably. 'What's so strange about it?' He wished people would mind their own business. The world seemed to be packed with imbeciles with nothing better to do with their time than gossip about the affairs of others.

'Nothing,' said Albert. 'With anyone other than yourself I'd be all for it, but – no offence old man – although the institution of marriage has much to commend it, I doubt its strictures suitable to a chap of your temperament.'

James scowled. 'I cannot for the life of me understand why a straightforward arrangement between Mr Biddulph and myself should be of the slightest concern to anyone but ourselves.'

'Mister Biddulph?' Albert stared. 'Dammit, man, you are not proposing to marry Mister Biddulph, but his daughter! What of the young lady? Did you propose to her, or to her father?'

The alliance was at Miss Biddulph's own suggestion,' said James stiffly.

'Alliance?' Albert clapped a hand to his forehead. 'Good God, you are marrying into coal!'

'And Biddulph,' said James, coldly, 'is marrying into shipping.'

Albert glanced at the portrait and smiled. 'I am sure that Anne would approve.'

James whitened with anger.

'I'm sorry, James,' Albert apologized contritely. 'I spoke hastily and lightly. Forgive me.'

'I'm to take me vows shortly,' Webster enunciated through a mouthful of kidney. He met their blank stares with a defiant air. 'And why not? I'm as much entitled to a morsel of companionship as the next man. And I'll not be marrying just to feather my nest. The Widow Malloy is as poor as a church mouse and will bring nothing but a few bits and pieces, but she has more character in her little finger than all your flibbertygibbets put together.'

'Congratulations,' said Albert weakly. 'When is the happy day?'

'As soon as maybe. At my age a man learns to be miserly with time, it is only the young who can afford to be spendthrift.' The rheumy eyes glowered at James. 'Ye need have no fear, I'll have my traps packed and my dunnage off the premises in good time.'

James blinked. 'What?'

'I'll give credit where credit's due. You've kept your bargain to the letter, but it did not include providing for two.'

'So that's it,' said James. 'Now listen to me, old man. When I gave my word to Anne it admitted of no equivocation. I promised to take care of you, and take care of you I shall. The fact that you have chosen to marry in no way releases me from that obligation. There is ample accommodation, and the more food eaten, the less the waste. So we'll say no more about it.'

'Most uncommon generous,' responded Webster gruffly. 'And I'm most uncommon grateful.' He dipped his head and returned to shovelling food into his mouth, but not before Albert and James had caught a glint of moisture beneath the drooping eyelids.

'You'll have your own quarters as usual,' said James. 'And no doubt your good lady will be able to make herself useful about the house.'

Webster choked over his food. 'I knew there'd be a catch to it! You never give without taking away!'

James grinned. The old man was happily back in his familiar role of cantankerous grouch.

Albert tucked his plans beneath his arm and turned to leave as the nurse – a plain, suet-faced woman, starched to the elbows – arrived, carrying Charlotte at arm's length, bathed and dressed for the morning inspection. He bent over the child, made soporific cooing noises, and winked at James. 'A typical Onedin. Solely concerned with her own comfort and oblivious to the world at large.' He took his leave and marched off cheerfully to his waiting carriage.

James pushed away his chair, stood up and stooped over his daughter. Experimentally he touched her nose. It felt like a piece of putty. Charlotte opened her eyes and promptly began to whimper and wail. James sighed. She was nothing but a weak, sickly, mewling girl-child. A strong healthy son was what he needed. He sniffed, grunted acknowledgment to the nurse, turned on his heel and set off for his office.

Webster left his end of the table and lumbered across. 'There, there, my little dumpling,' he purred. 'You deserve a better da than the one you've got.'

The child stopped its whimpering, blew bubbles of contentment and held out chubby arms.

'There, there,' said Webster and taking her from the nurse, began to walk up and down the room, rocking her gently and crooning softly, talking as much to himself as to the baby. 'There, there, my poor little Anne. Poor, poor little Anne.'

Elizabeth made her way to the docks. A fringed parasol hid her face from the sun, and her blushes from the catcalls and jibes from a few oafish bystanders. She had deliberated long into the night before finally giving way to temptation, but the bait had proved too irresistible to refuse. The picture of herself taking farewell of a lost love – just like Emily Hardaker in *The Emigrant's Return*, a dramatic presentation at which she had wept copiously when the distraught Miss Hardaker had declaimed 'Not all the portents of the heavens, nor the terrors of the raging seas shall keep us apart!', had added fuel to the fires of resolution.

Servants being notoriously prone to gossip, she had decided against taking the carriage, and had left the house at a sauntering walk with her heart beating painfully against her ribs at the thought of meeting Daniel alone and for the last time. He would almost certainly want to exchange kisses, and she occupied her mind during the walk to Canning Dock debating with herself whether to agree, and if so precisely what degree of intimacy would be permissible.

Having arrived at a conclusion satisfactory to herself she picked her way over the cobbles, past patient dray horses nuzzling feed bags, and threaded her way between stacks of packing cases and bales of cotton until she found herself facing the *Barracuda*.

The ship lay alongside, deep laden, sails neatly furled, hatches battened down and decks swept clear. Black hulled with white upperworks and teak handrails, she was obviously ready to put to sea. A tug, snuffling slowly through the open lock gates, shouldered aside a huddle of barges and panted into position at the bows.

Elizabeth paused a moment, caught sight of Daniel, smart in brass-buttoned uniform, standing on the poop deep in conversation with the pilot, then crossed the gangway with its pipe-clayed guard ropes to be handed down to the deck by a burly seaman in frayed guernsey and wide canvas trousers.

'This way, missus, if ye please. Cap'n's waiting.'

She steadied herself on the massive forearm, then Daniel, bearded face split into a grin of delight, dropped down the companionway and reached her in two long strides.

'I knew you'd come,' he exulted, unable to contain his delight. 'I knew it! We haven't much time, but . . .' He looked around, suddenly anxious. 'Where is the boy?'

The seaman had rolled away out of ear-shot. 'I couldn't possibly bring him, he's such a little gossip. You do understand?'

He wrung his big hands together and a worry-frown appeared on his forehead. 'But you promised,' he accused. 'You promised! I have the right. He is my son!'

She thought of Albert's dark suspicions. 'He would talk,' she repeated. 'Surely you can understand? How could I possibly explain?'

He nodded, defeated, accepting the inevitable. 'I should have thought of it, but. . . .' He pondered. 'I have made my decision and there is no going back. Come below and allow me to show you the accommodation.'

Her heart fluttered again as she obediently followed him along the deck to the housing beneath the poop. He opened the heavy teak door and invited her to proceed him down a short flight of carpeted stairs. Naturally he would want a few moments of privacy together, away from knowing eyes. She would, she decided, return his kiss, then shed a few tears before parting forever. It would be a quite romantic and bitter-sweet memory which she could hug to herself to her dying day.

The dining-saloon contained a table with three or four chairs, a massive sideboard with a brass rail surround and a fly-specked mirror, a long settee with leather upholstery, and was panelled with oak. It had an air of practicality, of spartan simplicity.

He quickly led the way across the saloon, opened a door, entered a short alleyway, turned right and, throwing open another door, stepped aside to allow her to enter.

The room took her breath away. It was sited at the stern, like a half moon, and stretched the full width of the ship. The panels were of pale green bordered with gold, and a semicircle of portholes bathed the room in pale milky light. The floor was thickly carpeted in a delicate shade of rose-pink, and a glass-fronted bookcase held an array of leather-bound volumes. There was a marble wash stand with a hinged top, a hip-bath, a small circular table with a brass rail surround, a pair of chintz-covered armchairs and a long settee with cushions of the same material. But the centre of attraction was undoubtedly the bed.

Elizabeth's eyes widened at the sight. It was of wrought iron curled into graceful arabesques, and each tie-rod was finished with a tiny rosette. The canopy was hung with extravagant folds of muslin, while the bedspread was fashioned of richly embroidered damask. At one side stood a circular marble-topped bedside cabinet with a bowl of fresh cut flowers, at the other a davenport of satinwood banded with rosewood.

Elizabeth caught her breath at the unexpected luxury. 'My,' she said at last. 'I never realized that ship's captains enjoyed such comfort.'

He shuffled uncomfortably, then jerked his thumb. 'My quarters are above. I meant this for you.'

She stared in disbelief. 'For me?'

He looked away from her curious feminine gaze and shrugged awkwardly. 'I had convinced myself – erroneously – that you would be coming with me.'

She was touched at this forethought. 'Oh, Daniel,' she murmured softly. 'You fool. You great booby,' and standing on tiptoes she leaned forward and kissed him gently on the mouth.

His arms encircled her waist and drew her towards him. She relaxed and, raising her arms, clasped her hands behind his neck, returning kiss for kiss. It was, she thought dreamily, a most satisfying conclusion and really quite, quite, romantic. She moved her head and a shadow slid across her vision. Then she distinctly felt the lift and fall of the ship as it freed itself from the restriction of the dock, and the shadow translated itself into the foot of one of the cranes sliding past the portholes.

She pulled herself away in a half-panic. 'Daniel! We – we are at sea!'

He held her at arm's length and smiled down, quite composed. 'Not yet. We must first pass through the lock before moving into the river. There is nothing to fear, you can go ashore with the pilot.' He grinned mischievously. 'Why? Did you imagine you were being shanghaied like some common fo'c'sle hand?'

Reassured by his humour she smiled back at him. 'I should love to sail out into the river. Do you know, I have never been aboard anything larger than a ferryboat before? Can I come up on deck and watch?'

He hesitated, then nodded agreement. 'Very well. But you must promise to keep out of the way. A ship is a busy world when preparing to put to sea, and seamen are not given to standing on ceremony. But you can join me on the poop deck if you wish, provided you stand well back and do not attempt to engage anyone in conversation.'

'I promise,' she said, aglow with excitement. This was to be a real adventure. The sort of thing which Anne had taken in her stride, and which had driven the unfortunate Emma mad.

She followed him up on to deck, and clambered the ladder to the poop deck.

It was a strange world which greeted her eyes. As the ship slid between the massive stone walls of the lock, men swarmed aloft like monkeys, and strung themselves out along the yards preparatory to loosing the sails, while the tug's paddles churned the oily water into mottled foam, and the hoarse-voiced pilot bawled incomprehensibilities to his counterpart on the tug.

The land glided past faster and faster until the bows, leaving the smooth water of the dock, met the swift run of the river. A mist of spray rose high above the foredeck to be blown away by an errant wind, and the jib flapped and boomed as it rattled up its stay.

As the tug sidled up-stream to keep the ship's head steady, the pilot turned towards Elizabeth and ventured politely: 'You are looking extremely well, Mrs Fogarty.'

Elizabeth, about to correct his misapprehension, hesitated, and thought the better of it. The pilot might have a wagging tongue, and heaven alone knew whom he might meet in the closed circle of the shipping community.

She smiled. 'I am keeping excellent health, thank you, Pilot.'

The pilot nodded to himself as though confirming a private diagnosis. 'The sea breezes will soon bring roses to your cheeks. I must say,' he added with clumsy gallantry. 'I envy Captain Fogarty his good fortune.'

A throaty whistle from the tug followed by choking cloud of black smoke put an end to the conversation. The pilot returned his attention to his duties, and a concerned Daniel hurried across as Elizabeth coughed and spluttered and wiped streaming eyes.

'You'd better go below for a few minutes, until we are in mid-stream.' Taking her arm he guided her down the companionway and back to the large cabin. 'I shall return in a few moments.' He paused at the door and grinned at her. 'You have a smut on your nose.'

As the door closed behind him she hurried to the mirror over the wash-stand to discover her face to be speckled with smuts. She poured water from a copper jug, found a tablet of soap, rinsed her hands and gave her face a quick cat-lick. A brand-new fluffy towel hung from the towel rail, and it was only when drying her hands that it occurred to her that the water was fresh, and the soap lying in its dish ready for instant use. She sniffed the air, discerning the faint odour of camphor and moth-balls and the merest hint of lavender.

A vague sense of unease prickled at the back of her mind. There was something odd, very odd about the situation. Daniel seemed to have put himself to a great deal of trouble for what at best could have been but a vain hope. Sniffing the air again Elizabeth followed her nose to a pair of brass-bound military chests standing shoulder to shoulder against one wall.

She pulled out a drawer and a froth of lace rose in protest against its close confinement. Filled with curiosity she dragged open the remaining drawers to discover them packed with feminine garments of every conceivable hue and colour. Blouses, skirts, petticoats. Fine linen. Boxes of cambric handkerchiefs. Silks and satins layered in tissue. He seemed to have thought of everything.

She turned away, puzzled by this almost obsessive attention to detail, then, glancing through the stern ports, saw the ship's wake creaming away through the broad ribbon of the river. At the same moment she became aware of a multitude of sounds which until now had barely penetrated her consciousness: the patter of bare feet, the rattle of yards, the boom of sails, hoarse commands, distant voices raised in a rhythmic chant, the purling run of water beneath the keel.

With her heart lurching into her throat she hurried to the door and tugged at the handle. The door was locked fast. In increasing panic she hammered with her fists, but built of solid teak it remained as unresponsive as though she were beating against a tree.

She turned away and ran to one of the portholes in time to see the tug drifting past, with the pilot standing on the bridge talking to the tug master. Feverishly she spun the two butterfly screws and swung the port glass open. She poked out her head and the wind howled and tore at her hair and tossed it into a wild mane.

The pilot looked up, saw her frantic face and waved an arm in cheerful farewell. Hysterically she began to scream for help. But the wind picked up her words and blew them to fragments. Only the gulls seemed to hear as they paced the ship on wide outspread wings and added their own cacophony of manic cries to the lone weak voice calling and calling in futile competition, until the ship, with canvas piled upon canvas, freed herself of the land and reached for the open sea.

CHAPTER ELEVEN

It was the pilot who unknowingly put them on the scent.

Baines,. idling his time while awaiting his next command, was taking his ease in the snug of the Steam Packet, enjoying a glass of hot spiced rum and a turn with a much-thumbed copy of *The Shipping Gazette*, when the pilot sauntered in, ordered a glass of brandy, caught Baines' eye, and rolled across to join him.

Baines, bored with his own company, put aside the news-sheet, and welcomed the intrusion with a beam of delight. Pilots were indefatigable gossips. They could talk at length of the strengths and weaknesses, the foibles and eccentricities of every master who sailed the seven seas. They were invaluable sources of information: which company carried which cargo, and to where. They took outward-bounders from the docks to the Bar, and returned with deep-laden ships whose canvas had been bleached by distant suns.

They knew each other of old and talked freely, as old campaigners will, while Baines set up another round and the conversation ran its elliptical course from the vagaries of wind and tide to the yawning gulfs of the oceans. They exchanged confidences and reminisced over past exploits and after toasting each other with a succession of increasingly large tots, came to the inevitable conclusion that the world was changing, and for the worse. They sentimentalized about the good old days before governmental edicts had bedevilled honest master mariners with Merchant Shipping Acts couched in lawyers' jargon, and commiserated with each other over the advent of steam.

'Damned contraptions,' snarled Baines. 'Falling-off-propellers and exploding engines. Banging and clattering day and night. There's no peace aboard a chimney-ship.'

The pilot nodded agreement. 'True, Cap'n Baines, very true. These days a lad still wet behind the ears can pull a lever and off she'll go against wind or tide. It's against nature, Cap'n Baines, against nature.'

'Give me a full-rigged ship with acres of canvas and a hearty crew, and I'll sail her to hell and back and show a profit,' said Baines. 'But these damned potato-choppers do naught but eat coal and spew out soot like floating factories. They're stuffed with machinery and manned by Paddy Doyle firemen.'

The pilot hiccuped and gave his chest an admonitory thump. 'Ugly brutes. Dirty as sin and built like barrels. Fit only for emigrants and livestock. They'll never complete with Cape Horners. Like the one I took out only yesterday morning. The *Barracuda*. A Callon boat. Ship-rigged and a treat to the eye. Commanded by young Fogarty. D'you know him?'

Baines nodded. 'Taking her out himself, did you say?'

'Cleared for Melbourne, Australia.'

'The devil, you say.' Baines frowned, perplexed. 'But he has not long since inherited the company.'

The pilot shrugged. 'Be that as it may, he is also taking a young wife with him. Pretty as a picture for all that she was reported to be of delicate constitution.'

'The last voyage almost drove her out of her wits.' Baines shook his big head. 'I don't understand it.'

'I've always maintained that a wife's place is beneath her husband.' The pilot nudged Baines and winked knowingly. 'There'll be many a transit of Venus taken during that voyage, I'll warrant.'

Baines sat silent, mulling over the information through a fog of alcohol. If the pair had set sail for Australia, then who remained to look after the interests of the company? Baffled, he decided that this was a nut upon which Mr Onedin could test his teeth. 'Drink up,' he said to the pilot. 'Swallow that down and have another.

A restless and distraught Albert was pacing James' office and chewing at his fingernails as Baines lurched in redolent with the aroma of rum.

'I can't think,' said Albert for the hundredth time. 'I just can't think. . . .'

'I can,' said James. He steepled his fingers and considered carefully. 'She left home yesterday morning, leaving no word, taking nothing with her, and nothing has been seen of her since.'

'I have had servants out scouring the town, I have inquired at hospitals. Nothing. She has simply disappeared.'

'Jewellery?'

'What?'

James explained patiently. 'If Elizabeth left her jewellery behind, you may be sure she had every intention of returning.' He finally took notice of Baines swaying unsteadily in the middle of the room. 'Yes? What is it?' he demanded irritably.

The giant licked his lips with a tongue that felt as thick as a fur coat, and spoke with the laboured care of a man picking his way through a labyrinth. 'Dan'l Fogarty has sailed wi' the *Barracuda* for Australia. I got the information from the pilot. Thought you'd be innerested.' he hiccuped gravely.

'You're drunk,' said James.

Baines nodded agreeably. 'In the way o' duty. Cost me a bottle o' rum and . . .' He hup-hupped again. 'That pilot drinks brandy like mother's milk. But it loosed his tongue. He also said that Fogarty had his wife aboard.'

'Damn Fogarty and his affairs,' said Albert. 'I've troubles enough of my own.'

'Wait a moment,' said James. 'Daniel and Emma Fogarty have left for Australia, together?'

'That's what the pilot said.' Baines fell into a chair and breathed stertorously.

'But if they have sailed together, who is to run the company?'

'Exactly,' said Baines. 'That's exactly my reasoning. They'll be selling off their ships.'

James shook his head. 'It doesn't make sense. No one could dispose of a company as quickly as that. As for Emma sailing with him . . .' He knitted his brows, perplexed. 'I can't believe it. The last voyage almost deprived her of her reason.'

'The pilot had heard the same story. Said he was surprised to find her looking so well.'

'He actually saw her aboard?'

'Spoke with her for a few moments. Then she went below. The last he saw of her was after they cast off the tug. She was leaning out of one of the lower ports and waving farewell.'

James shook his head, baffled. 'I don't understand it. The pilot is quite positive it was Emma?'

'Well, he said it was Mrs Fogarty.' Baines shrugged. 'Who else could it be?'

James and Albert looked at each other, the same thought crossing their minds.

'Oh, no!' said Albert desperately. 'No! It couldn't be! She wouldn't . . .!'

'We must not leap to hasty conclusions,' said James. He returned his attention to Baines. 'Had the pilot ever met Mrs Fogarty before yesterday?'

Baines scratched his poll. 'I dunno. I'm not certain sure, but I had the impression it was the first time he'd set eyes on her.'

'Did he describe her?'

'Not exactly. Just remarked that she was as pretty as a picture and seemed to be in prime health. She had a parasol and walked to the ship. Come aboard just afore she was due to cast off.'

James and Albert exchanged glances once again, with the same unspoken thought. Emma would never walk unescorted through the dock area.

'Well,' said James, at length. 'We shall soon settle it, one way or the other.' He rang the bell for Tupman. 'I shall pay a call. If Emma is at home . . .' He left the sentence unfinished.

'I'll kill him,' said Albert. 'I'll hunt him down and kill him.'

'You'll need to catch him first,' James commented dryly. 'And he has a head start and a fast ship.'

Albert bared his teeth. 'She's my wife.'

'That gives you prior claim,' said James. 'But she is also my sister, and I think I know her as well as anyone can know the vagaries of a woman. Elizabeth may be wayward and as temperamental as a race horse, but she's no fool. There's more to this than meets the eye, Albert.'

Tupman, James' chief clerk, entered, his waxen face as expressionless as ever.

'Ah, Mr Tupman. How quickly could you get me a copy of the *Barracuda*'s clearance papers? I want to know her cargo, ports of call, and her crew list with particular attention as to whether any passengers or supernumeraries are carried.'

Tupman reflected a moment. 'I believe Mr Agnew would oblige me. Could you give me an hour, sir?'

'That would do admirably, Tupman, thank you,' said James.

The clerk bowed himself out and James glanced at the other two. Baines was snoring peacefully and Albert had changed from chewing his fingernails to gnawing his knuckles. James' brain always worked at its best when faced with a difficult and complicated problem. His mind carefully weighed pros and cons, accepted and rejected, until a course of action seemed clear. Trade. Trade was the key. If Fogarty had abandoned the company, he must be desperately short of money. He would follow the trade winds and make a killing at each port. In his mind's eye he traversed the oceans, selecting and discarding. Fogarty was an experienced master, but he lacked imagination. He would stick to Callon ports and Callon agents. Once lay his hands upon the *Barracuda*'s cargo manifest and he would be able to plot the *Barracuda*'s course as though he were laying off her charts himself. The immediate problem was Albert. Unless that young man was given something to keep him occupied, he would go to pieces.

James coughed for attention. 'Perhaps you should call upon Robert and Sarah. Elizabeth may have paid them a visit, stayed overnight, or been taken ill. There is probably a quite simple explanation.'

'She would have notified me, sent a message,' said Albert, dully.

'Messages go astray, and servants are not always reliable.' It was a weak excuse, but Albert was a man clutching at straws.

'I'll go immediately,' he said, and reached for his hat.

James waited for the door to close behind him, then sent for his carriage and, with a parting glance at the slumbering Baines, left for the Callon mansion.

Emma received him in the drawing-room and held out a letter. 'He's gone,' she replied woodenly in answer to his inquiry.

James carried the letter to the shaded window and held it up to the light.

> 'Dear Wife' [he read]. 'Pressure of business calls me away for an indefinite period. I have made full provision for your future in accordance with your late father's wishes, and you may draw upon our bankers for any sum you may immediately require. Agnew is more than capable of taking care of the business during my absence and I advise that you be guided by his experience. I am sure that he will put your interests before all other. I also deposited with our lawyers a document giving you free and unfettered control of your inheritance. You should be able to live comfortably from the income or, if you should decide to sell, from the interest on invested capital. I will concur whatever your decision. The company is rightfully yours, and all I have taken as my share is one vessel, the *Barracuda*.
>
> You will now be your own mistress, and I am sure that you will agree that a prolonged period of separation can but serve to heal the breach between us.
>
> I remain,
> Your most affectionate husband,
> Daniel'

'The man's a fool,' said James, returning the letter.

'But what does it mean?' Emma looked at him anxiously as though hoping a second opinion would re-interpret the brutal truth.

'It means,' said James bluntly. 'That your husband has sailed for Australia and has not the slightest intention of returning.'

'But why?' she wailed. 'Why?'

James shrugged. 'I have no idea.'

She hugged her thin shoulders and rocked her head in an excess of misery. 'I haven't been a good wife to him. I haven't been a good wife.'

'His actions are hardly those of a model husband,' James commented dryly. 'But at least he has left one sound piece of advice. Sell. Sell without delay.'

She looked up, a flare of suspicion in her eyes. 'To you, I suppose? I know you, James Onedin, for a man never to allow an opportunity to pass, but I never imagined that even you could behave as vilely as this.'

'I don't want the company,' said James. 'Nor any part of it. I have other plans nearing fulfilment.' It was nothing but the plain truth, he thought, quietly exultant, for Fogarty's hare-brained action had successfully destroyed his nearest and most powerful competitor. Under the circumstances he could afford to be charitable.

'I am sorry,' said Emma. 'Please forgive me for doubting your motives which I am sure spring from a generous heart, but you will readily understand that I am somewhat distraught.'

'Sell,' James repeated. 'As quickly as possible, but not piece-meal. Put the company up for offer as a going concern but retain a half interest for yourself.'

She looked at him, suddenly acquisitive. 'Could I do that?'

'Nothing easier,' said James. 'There's plenty of ready money about. Consult your lawyers, of course, but that would be my advice.'

Emma considered for a moment. 'I know so little of business matters. Would it not be better to first make a private approach?'

Before the wolves can gather to pick at your bones, thought James. Emma, he decided, was of true Callon stock and, behind that air of helpless femininity, as sharp as a weasel.

'You might try Frazers,' he suggested. 'You may remember meeting father and son at dinner the other night, so further introduction would be unnecessary.' And Albert on the board would give him another iron in the fire. Yes, if she and Frazers could be persuaded to nibble at the bait he might be able to hook an even larger fish. His brain worked quickly. An exchange of shares, Onedin for Callon and Biddulph for Frazer, could extend his interests into both ship-building and coal.

'Frazers?' The deep violet eyes were as guileless as twin pools. 'I understood that they were engaged solely in the occupation of ship building?'

James' estimate of her shrewdness rose. She was worth a dozen Daniel Fogarty's. 'They have ample capital, but their yards are hemmed in by docks and cannot be extended further. Jack Frazer is a man with a keen eye for a bargain, and also has the reputation of being somewhat susceptible to the charms of the weaker sex.'

She filed away the information, expressed her gratitude for his sympathy and advice, dabbed at an imaginary tear, and planned to write immediately to Mr Frazer.

James bowed himself out and concluded that there was nothing like the smell of money to banish the odour of tragedy. He swung cheerfully down the gravelled drive to his waiting carriage, whistling contentedly. All in all, he considered, he had put a half hour's conversation to good use.

Sarah was entertaining Leonora and Cousin Richard to tea when Albert was announced.

He took his allotted place, perched a plate of cucumber sandwiches on one knee, a cup of tea on the other, and showed polite interest in the idle prattle while his brain seethed with anxiety and he sought for an opportunity to broach the subject uppermost in his mind.

The lull came at last. 'Have you spoken with Elizabeth lately?' he asked Sarah, elaborately unconcerned.

'Not since our little dinner party,' answered Sarah. Her eyes sharpened and she leaned forward, always avid for gossip. 'Why? Did you expect to find her here?'

'No, no,' Albert assured her. 'It is simply that she went for a walk – a morning constitutional – and I made the assumption – obviously false – that she might have made her way here.'

'A walk?' Sarah, on the scent of scandal, pounced like a cat.

'Elizabeth would never walk as far as this. She would take a carriage.'

Albert privately cursed himself for a slip of the tongue, and realized that two sleepless nights had addled his wits. 'The fact is,' he said, abandoning all pretence. 'I'm rather concerned. She seems to have disappeared.'

'Disappeared?' It was evident that Sarah could not believe her ears that all her direst prognostications were being fulfilled. She leaned even further forward. 'You must be exaggerating, Albert. She has been out shopping and lost track of time.'

'That I'm afraid is not possible.' Albert thought he intercepted an exchange of glances between Leonora and Richard. He therefore addressed his remarks directly to them. 'I should be grateful for any information which might throw light on the mystery.' The cup and saucer chattered on his knee. 'It really is most disturbing.'

Leonora could contain herself no longer. 'She wouldn't!' she exclaimed. 'She swore she wouldn't! We overheard them, didn't we, Richard?'

Richard tried ineffectually to stop her, but Leonora, once in full spate was as impossible to dam as a river that had burst its banks.

'We quite by chance overheard a conversation between Mr Fogarty and, and . . .'

'Cousin Elizabeth,' said Richard.

'Yes. Well, we were not eavesdropping, you understand? But we were in a position of some delicacy in that we could not divulge our presence without giving away the fact that we had been privy to their exchange of confidences. Naturally our lips were sealed, and neither of us would dream of repeating a word, would we, Richard?' She clutched Richard's hand for support, Sarah licked her lips in anticipation of a juicy morsel of scandal, and Albert ground his teeth and wished the damned chatterbox would come to the point.

'Quite. None of our business,' Cousin Richard interposed briefly.

Albert held back his temper and addressed himself to Richard. 'Perhaps you would take upon yourself the burden of explanation and save Miss Biddulph further embarrassment?'

'Certainly,' said Richard. 'Cousin Elizabeth and Mr Fogarty were engaged in a somewhat intemperate argument. It was my impression that they had a relationship of long-standing. Nothing improper,' he added hastily. 'Miss Biddulph will bear me out – there was never the slightest hint of impropriety.'

Leonora squeezed his hand and nodded earnest affirmation.

'It was simply that Mr Fogarty told Cousin Elizabeth of his decision to sail for Australia and never return and he . . .'

Sarah could contain herself no longer. 'Daniel Fogarty leaving for the Antipodes? Alone?' This was a veritable feast of information. And under her own roof!

Richard looked straight at Albert. 'That, at least, he made abundantly clear. He would be sailing alone. But he begged and pleaded, was most insistent that Cousin Elizabeth paid a visit to the ship on sailing day to bid farewell. Frankly, I found the fellow's attitude quite overbearing. A most stormy argument developed.'

'Did my wife accede?' demanded Albert, nerves stretched to breaking point.

'Not at first,' said Richard, choosing his words with care. 'At first she refused absolutely, reminding him that it would be quite improper for a lady to venture unescorted to so insalubrious an area as the waterfront; but eventually, after renewed pleas and exhortations, she temporized. Held out no promises, mark you. It is my belief that she desired nothing other than to put an end to a distressing conversation. I so assure you Mr Frazer, that Cousin Elizabeth's behaviour throughout was beyond reproach – as was that of Mr Fogarty, in spite of his boorishness.'

'Nevertheless, she did visit the ship,' said Albert coldly.

'We cannot be certain.'

'I can,' said Albert. He carefully placed cup and saucer by the side of his chair, flicked a crumb from his jacket, rose to his full height and, with habitual courtesy, apologized for taking up their time. Then bowing to Sarah and Leonora, he walked stiff-faced from the room.

Leonora patted Richard's hand. 'I thought you handled that remarkably well, Richard.'

Richard took out a handkerchief and mopped his brow. 'I

thought so too. And do you know? – I never s-stammered once.'

'Dear Richard,' said Leonora fondly.

Sarah twisted her features into a confidential smile. 'Now you really must tell me all, dear Leonora. I am agog to hear every word.'

Leonora was more than a match for Sarah. The brown eyes widened in artless innocence. 'But we have told all, Mrs Onedin. Both dear Richard and myself are deeply concerned that there should be no misapprehension. Particularly as the unhappy circumstance took place beneath your roof. I mean, it is unthinkable that so much as the merest breath of scandal should touch your household. We must remember,' she added ingenuously. 'That there is your husband's position to consider. Members of the Chamber of Commerce are such a stuffy lot, don't you agree?'

Richard gave Leonora's hand a congratulatory squeeze as the shaft went home, and Sarah primped her lips to nod her head in vigorous agreement. 'Not another word, I beg of you. My ears are closed.'

'I do so appreciate your confidence, Mrs Onedin,' said Lenora, demurely. 'You see, we were in the conservatory at the time, and should the secret be mooted abroad I should be most dreadfully compromised.' She smiled fondly into Richard's alarmed face. 'Dear Richard is such a fearful spoon.'

She must be mad, thought Richard. Quite, quite mad. Now nothing would stop Sarah's tongue from wagging. The knowledge would come to Biddulph's ears and . . . He looked at Leonora with new respect. The cunning little minx, he thought. The clever, cunning little minx.

Albert refilled his glass from James' decanter and stared gloomily at his outstretched feet. 'It's as plain as the nose on your face. She's left me. Left me for that oafish lout. The whole business was planned. Planned in detail. Must have been.'

'Planned by Fogarty, but not by Elizabeth,' said James.

They were seated in James' drawing-room, the fire spitting sparks from smouldering logs, while Albert concentrated upon the task of drinking himself into insensibility.

'She must have been party to it. She was on deck. The pilot

spoke to her. There was nothing to prevent her demanding to be put ashore.' Albert gulped his brandy and kicked morosely at one of the logs. The log spluttered angrily and sent yellow flames twisting up the chimney.

'I have shanghaied many a man in my time,' said James. 'It is not as difficult as you think. True, by allowing her on deck, Fogarty took a risk. But only a slight one. Remember, the pilot imagined he was speaking to Mrs Fogarty. It only required Daniel to remark that his unfortunate wife had not fully recovered from a derangement of the mind for any outburst to be treated as further proof.'

'But the pilot would be bound to talk.'

'He did,' James reminded him. 'But once on the high seas no amount of gossip would bring them back. Fogarty is safe from hue and cry. Or so he imagines.'

'If the brute really has kidnapped her . . .!' Albert blanched at the inescapable conclusion. 'She will be entirely at his mercy!'

'If I know Elizabeth,' said James. 'Daniel Fogarty will quickly discover that he has caught a tiger by the tail.'

CHAPTER TWELVE

The *Barracuda* left Liverpool with a soldier's wind and six days later dropped anchor in the Tagus.

The River of Straw flowed like molten gold and Lisbon rose in serrated white terraces to the old castle of São Jorge perched high above the city. But there was no time for sight-seeing, for Daniel had planned carefully and telegraphed ahead.

Within the space of six hours the *Barracuda* had taken on a dozen casks of olive oil, ten pipes of port wine and two hundred cases of Bacalhau, the famous salted cod of Portugal. Then she hauled up and fled for the open sea.

The loading had not gone unnoticed. Senhor Braganza, alerted by a telegraph from James, had despatched one of his clerks to take notes of the *Barracuda*'s business, and even as the ship was shaking out its sails the information was relayed to Senhor Onedin in Liverpool.

Daniel waited until the white crenellated Tower of Belem dropped astern and the bows were lifting to the long rolling swell of the Atlantic then, followed by the sympathetic gaze of the crew, squared his shoulders and made his way below to face an Elizabeth who this far had won every round of the battle.

On leaving Liverpool he had left her alone until the sun had set and a dust of stars had sprinkled the sky, before venturing to tap at the door, turn the key and enter the room.

He had expected tears and remonstrances but was quite unprepared for the tempest of fury that had met his overtures.

She had screeched like a fishwife, bombarded him with books, shoes, hairbrushes; everything portable upon which she could lay her hands. The room was a wreck. She had dragged out drawers, opened cupboards, piled the contents in the middle of the floor, and now threatened to set fire to the lot and burn the ship about his ears unless he immediately turned back. However, as she lacked the means of striking a light, he was able to beat a retreat and leave her to weep alone in the dark.

The following morning he had essayed a second attempt, taking as a peace offering a breakfast tray of cold chicken, freshly baked bread and a pot of coffee, reasoning that by now she must be ravenously hungry. He had straightened an overturned table and put down the tray, at the same time repeatedly assuring her that she had nothing to fear from him, that her person was, and would remain, inviolate, that he loved her to distraction and that his sole purpose in abducting her was in order that they may make a new start together in distant Australia.

She had responded to these protestations with an unladylike snarl, picked up the tray and hurled the contents at his head.

On the third day she had succumbed to a bout of sea-sickness and lay abed, moaning and groaning as the stern rose and fell and the deck canted steeply, while the ship ploughed across the endless rollers of Biscay. He had allowed her heavings and retchings to go unnoticed and taken the opportunity to tidy the room, neatly folding and replacing the garments into drawers and boxes, It was only when picking up the shattered crockery that he realized that hunger must have overcome fortitude, for the bread was missing and the chicken had been picked to the bone. He had then tactfully tip-toed out without a backward glance, leaving recovery to the balm of time.

Two days later she was on her feet again and, although berating him as soundly as ever, showed an inclination to talk. Not that it was much of a conversation, rather a series of questions and answers. Where exactly was the ship? When could it be expected to reach port? Which port? Could she go on deck for a breath of fresh air? Could she go ashore to do some shopping? The naïvety of the last question had brought a smile to his lips which had thrown her into a fresh paroxysm of fury.

Daniel made his way along the alleyway, tapped at her door, waited until a waspish voice bade him enter, then took the key from his pocket and turned the lock.

She had brushed and combed and pinned her hair and changed into a pale green crinoline, striped stockings and tiny satin bootees. She summoned up a dissembling smile. 'As it is obviously your intention to keep me prisoner until we reach our destination, I think, Captain Fogarty, that it is high time we reached an accommodation.'

Daniel winced at the formal use of his name, but agreed eagerly. At least it seemed that she was now prepared to accept the inevitable and adapt herself to circumstances.

'To that end,' she continued. 'I would be prepared to meet your officers. I would suggest at dinner tonight.'

He had been prepared for such an eventuality, for he could hardly keep her below decks and out of sight for the duration of the voyage. 'On one condition,' he told her. 'I must have your promise that you will never disclaim that you are anyone other than Mrs Fogarty.'

She shook her head vehemently. 'Never! Such mendacity would condemn me utterly!'

'I do not ask that you introduce yourself as my wife, merely that you do not deny it. Furthermore,' he added, playing his trump card. 'Should you do so, you will not be believed.' He considered that he had handled that very possibility with the cunning of a Machiavelli. On leaving Liverpool he had put on the gloomy expression of a man at his wit's end and, well within earshot of the helmsman, had taken the Mate into his confidence, outlining the story of Emma's voyage to China, and impressing upon the taciturn Mr Kennedy that his dear wife was still suffering from a disorder of the mind, in consequence of which she had a tendency towards irrational outbursts of rage. Also that the recent death of her father had so unbalanced the poor demented creature that she suffered from confusions of identity, sometimes imagining herself to be one person, sometimes another. Mr Kennedy had listened sympathetically, while the helmsman had pricked up his ears eager to retail this juicy morsel of gossip to his shipmates. From that moment forward Elizabeth's storms of anger and pleas for help had simply elicited a grave wagging of heads and exchanges of know-it-all looks from officers and crew alike.

Elizabeth listened in disbelief to his explanation. 'It is not Emma who is mad,' she declared. 'It is you. You have quite taken leave of your senses.'

He smiled agreeably. 'I would prefer to describe myself as bewitched, for it is commonly held that those pierced by Cupid's arrows are invariably driven out of their wits. The pipes of Pan subjugate all to his will.'

She looked into the obsessive eyes of the true madman, and for the first time began to experience the reality of fear. Until this moment she had been irrationally convinced that Daniel was no more than a ridiculous figure of fun and, given time and a display of obstinacy, could be turned from his purpose. She had time to wonder how one of her favourite heroines would act given the same circumstances. Swoon, in all probability. Those insipid creatures were much given to swooning and then recovering none the worse for the experience. But, she thought bitterly, the ships and towers in which they found themselves confined were of cardboard and the villain unmasked himself at the conclusion; and no doubt later shared oysters and stout with the heroine in some seedy boarding house.

'You are living in a world of imagination, Daniel,' she told him gently. 'Go to Australia. Make your fortune. But put me ashore before it is too late.'

He smiled his madman's smile. 'If you are of the same mind

when we reach Melbourne I will put you aboard the next homeward bound ship. I promise. In the meantime you have naught to fear from me. I give you my word.'

'Don't you understand?' she pleaded desperately. 'I can never be your wife. We have gone our separate ways. It is too late to turn back the clock.'

'In England, yes. In Australia no. There we can live as man and wife, with none the wiser. Believe me, Elizabeth, you shan't regret it. We shall put the clock back and make a new beginning.'

'Albert will seek us out. He will never give up. He will hunt you down. Albert is not a forgiving man.'

'That ninny! He couldn't find a chicken in a henhouse. He's nothing but an armchair designer. What does he know of the sea and ships?'

'Very little,' she admitted. 'But you are forgetting James.'

'James?'

'You have abducted his sister, and my brother is even less forgiving than Albert. In your shoes I should think twice about crossing swords with such an adversary. Elizabeth tried to sound confident, but realized dismally that it was an empty threat. One of James' more infuriating characteristics was his studied aloofness from the affairs of others.

Daniel seemed to read her mind. 'James? James would never so much as help a blind beggar across a road unless he could see a profit in it.'

James called upon Emma. 'I want you to sell me the *Barracuda,*' he stated without preliminary. 'At a nominal figure of course. Shall we say five hundred pounds?'

Emma stared, bewildered. 'The *Barracuda*? But the *Barracuda* is no longer in my possession, Mr Onedin. Surely you must be aware of the fact?'

'I am,' said James. 'But all I require is that you make out a bill of sale and leave the rest to me.'

Emma considered. 'You seem to be in a most intemperate haste to buy a pig in a poke, Mr Onedin. May I ask why?'

'Time is short,' said James. 'And let us say that you are not alone in having a score to settle with Daniel Fogarty.'

'That ship is worth every penny of £12,000,' said Emma thoughtfully.

'But not to you. To you, she is worthless. I take the risk and therefore expect the reward.'

'And what of my reward? Am I to be the loser yet again?'

'Revenge,' said James.

She nodded her head. 'He should not be allowed to go unpunished. I take it that you would want the bill of sale predated?'

James shook his head. 'Nothing underhand. Today's date will do admirably. And have it countersigned by your lawyer.'

'Very well, Mr Onedin, I agree. Then what will you do?'

'Find him.'

'But the oceans are so vast.' For a moment a shadow of old terrors flitted across her features. 'I had no idea how vast.'

'They are also empty,' said James. 'I intend to catch him in port.'

Albert read Braganza's cable then tossed it aside. 'What does it mean?'

James sighed at the young man's obtuseness. 'It means exactly what it says: Olive oil for the Azores, dried fish for Spanish Town, wine for the Brazils.'

Albert looked blank, so James tried again. 'We know from the *Barracuda*'s manifest that she was putting into Lisbon to off-load half a dozen cases of glassware. It seemed unlikely that an experienced a master as Fogarty would miss the opportunity of taking on a few parcels, so I sent a telegraph to my old friend Senhor Braganza. Fogarty will sail with the trade winds and show a profit on the way.'

Albert brightened. 'If we start immediately we could head him off at the Azores.'

'Not so quickly,' said James. 'In the first place, I have but four ships and they are fully engaged.'

'I'll charter a vessel,' said Albert promptly.

'You can do better than that,' said James. 'I have had a talk with Emma. The poor creature is at her wit's end. Fogarty has signed and deposited with her lawyers, a document in which he relinquishes all control of the company and leaves it entirely to her. Lock, stock and barrel.'

'So?'

'That company is now like a ship without a rudder. I am sure it would take very little persuasion for Emma to sell.' James rubbed his hands together. 'It will go for a song.'

Albert stared. 'You intend to buy out Callon and Company?'

'Not me. You.'

'Me?' Albert's stare changed to one of utter disbelief. 'You expect me to take advantage of that poor woman's distress? And to what end?'

'Initially,' said James. 'To rescue your wife. Ultimately to turn a fat profit. Even you cannot be averse to turning an honest penny.'

'An honest penny!' Albert came to his feet and paced angrily about the room. He ran a hand through his hair. 'Can't you understand the enormity of what you are suggesting? That unfortunate, demented creature. . . .'

'That unfortunate demented creature,' James interrupted coolly. 'Will live to bless the day you approached her. You are not thinking clearly, Albert. I have often commented upon the fact that people in the grip of sentiment tend to lose all sense of reality.' He surveyed Albert with a deceptively mild avuncular gaze, pulled at his nose, then steepling his fingers, leaned back in his chair. 'Unless Emma disposes of her property at a favourable price, she will assuredly be bankrupt within a matter of months. There will be plenty ready to take advantage of her ignorance. What does she know of shipping? She will be robbed by clerks, exploited by agents, rooked by shipmasters, preyed upon by the unscrupulous. Does your conscience not extend to holding out a helping hand?'

'I protest you really are the most plausible rogue I have ever had the misfortune to meet,' Albert complained irascibly. 'I will have no part of it. Even could I afford so high an investment.'

'There speaks a man who measures charity by the weight of his wallet,' James observed cynically. 'Put the proposal to your father. He'll not allow sentiment to stand in the way of business.'

'My father?' Albert sounded incredulous.

'If Callon's go to pot he will be the first to suffer. Once sold, the fleet will be scattered far and wide, and there will be no more new ships on the stocks, no more repair work.'

'My father is hardly likely to buy into a failing company for the privilege of nailing planks into the sides of rotting hulks,' said Albert with some asperity.

'The finest sailing vessels on the western ocean can hardly be described as rotting hulks,' James commented mildly. 'Let me put it to you like this: You are in the position of buying into a profitable business with a comparatively small outlay. Suggest to your father that you share the costs. Offer Emma a half interest. Go limited, with Emma as a sleeping partner.

Albert paused in his restless pacing. 'You expect her to sell at half value?' He shook his head firmly. 'She would never agree.'

'She will if you make the right approach. Emma has been protected all her life. Now, with her father dead, abandoned by her husband, she needs the promise of security – and what greater finanacial security could she ask than a guarantee by Frazers?'

'Your argument has not changed,' said Albert coldly. 'You are still demanding that I take advantage of a defenceless woman.'

'While you are debating with your conscience,' James reminded him testily. 'There is another defenceless woman out on the high seas. Dammit, Albert, I am offering you the opportunity of retrieving your wife and showing a profit into the bargain. What more do you want?'

Albert expelled a breath of exasperation. James was James, and nothing would change him. The man was obviously a stranger to the sensibilities which guided the rest of humanity. Even with his sister in mortal danger he had to plot and scheme, bend others to his will.

'I don't see where this is leading. You have never shown any altruistic motives before, so where lies your gain?'

'Ah,' said James. 'I was coming to that. We detach a Callon ship. The *Firefly* has completed discharging and is lying idle awaiting a cargo. She is one of Callon's fastest clippers, and with a load of salt and cotton goods could make the passage to

Jamaica in short time. We'll trap Fogarty in Spanish Town. I'll put Baines in command, he is the best blue water master you could hope to find, and we shall sail together, for I, too, have a bone to pick with Fogarty. I impose but one condition: If I get Elizabeth back, safe and sound, you give me the *Firefly*.'

Albert gaped and emitted a strangulated gurgle. 'You have the cool effrontry to demand a ship in payment for Elizabeth's safety!'

James raised an amused eyebrow. 'What value do you set upon the safe return of your wife? Even knights of old were expected to pay for their armour.'

'You really pass all human understanding.' Albert paused. 'Very well. I shall speak to father. But that is all I can promise.'

'It will be enough,' said James. 'Iron Jack Frazer has his head screwed on the right way. He will take little persuasion.'

'Even so,' Albert protested. 'There will be no time. These matters cannot be settled in a few minutes.'

'A letter of intent is all that is necessary. You can safely leave the rest to me.'

'I believe you,' said Albert bitterly. 'You would shake hands with the Devil for a profit.'

'Why not?' asked James equably. 'At least the Devil has the reputation of looking after his own.' He eyed Albert speculatively. The man was obviously unwell and the tension showed. 'I think perhaps we should speak to your father together.'

'I wish you would,' said Albert. 'I am no match for him. I never was.'

'Does he know of Elizabeth's disappearance?'

'He knows nothing. This will come as a shock to him.'

'Then we shan't enlighten him.' James took the decision for both. 'We shall simply tell him that Fogarty has left the country, and Emma wishes to sell. That should be surprise enough for any man.'

Mr Frazer sat in his creaking leather chair, filling the room with clouds of cigar smoke, and listening without interruption to their recital.

Then he nodded slowly.

'I have had a communication from Mrs Fogarty, requesting the favour of a few minutes' conversation. I must admit that I was somewhat at a loss to understand its purport until this moment.' He sighed. 'Poor George Callon. He must be turning in his grave. He had such high hopes. Looked upon young Fogarty as a son. And treated him as such.' The granite face twisted into bitter lines and a big hand clinched gnarled joints into a fist. He looked directly at Albert. 'A man builds his life on hope, but the young have a habit of turning old men's dreams to ashes.'

'Callon's have carried you for years!', Albert exclaimed hotly. 'Without my side of the business to support you, your yard would be empty!'

The fist crashed upon the desk. 'You're on about bloody steam again! I build the finest clippers in the port!'

'Only because of lack of competition. Everyone else is turning to steam.'

Father and son glared at one another. The father recovered first. 'So,' he asked softly. 'You are inviting me to put good money into an undertaking which you believe doomed to failure? Why?' He switched his gaze to James. 'Are you at the bottom of this, Onedin?'

'I think,' said James judiciously. 'That Albert sometimes allows enthusiasm to run away with his tongue. The days of sail are probably coming to an end; but not in your lifetime, and I doubt in mine. In the meantime there will be trade enough for both. They are obverse sides to the same coin.'

'No doubt,' Frazer commented dryly. 'But you have carefully avoided answering my question. What part are you playing, Onedin?'

'Mrs Fogarty did me the honour of taking me into her confidence,' James replied obliquely.

'And your first thought was to come rushing round to Frazers? There's more to it than that.'

James shrugged. 'Mrs Fogarty asked my advice, and I gave it. If you are not interested I will simply suggest she looks elsewhere.' He dipped beneath his chair and picked up his hat.

'Now don't let us be overhasty. This is something a man cannot rush into. It requires thought.'

James brushed the nap of his hat. 'Don't take too long. News travels quickly.'

'Perhaps I'd best call on her.' Frazer ruminated for a few moments. 'Aye that might be best. Meet her in her own home. She'll feel more at ease over a dish of tea. A man's place of business is bound to put a woman at a disadvantage.' Unconsciously his hand had moved to adjust his tie.

'She is quite a good-looker,' said James, winking at Albert.

'What the devil are you implying?' roared Frazer. 'I have known Emma Callon since she was a babe.'

No doubt, reflected James, but long acquaintanceship did not necessarily cool a man's ardour, and Frazer's protest had been delivered with rather too much vehemence for a man who pretended no more than an avuncular interest. He squirreled away the knowledge for future use. 'I am sure you will treat the lady with all civility,' he said tactfully.

The old man grunted, then the craggy face tormented itself into a knowing grin. 'If one half of what I hear is true, it would seem that you have not been above plying your oar in a certain direction?'

James' nose pinched with anger, and he was only interrupted from a sharp rejoinder by a deprecatory cough from Albert.

'I think, father, we should keep to the business in hand.'

Frazer tugged at his side-whiskers. 'I could set it up as a subsidiary, feed the profits into the yards . . . On the other hand Callon's business has been falling off lately . . . It requires thought. A deal of thought.'

'Why not come in with me?' asked James mildly.

'Come in with you? By God, I knew it! I knew there could be no show without Punch!'

'Now don't go off at half-cock.' James smiled affably. 'I am not about to suggest anything out of the ordinary. If I had capital to spare I'd venture to take up a few shares; but I haven't. I am putting every penny I can scrape together into four new steamships to be built by Albert.'

'So?'

'Coaling stations. We start with the Cape Verdes.'

Frazer's thick brows knitted to leave a pair of deep furrows above the bridge of his nose. 'What?'

'A steamship making a long passage needs somewhere to bunker. Albert builds steamers. I can obtain coal at rock bottom prices, your ships could carry coal out and cargo back. We shall feed off each other and show a profit.'

'I'll not grow fat on supplying four or five ships.'

'Where one leads, others will follow. I envisage a chain of coaling stations, strategically placed, and controlled by Frazer-Onedin.'

Frazer eyed James shrewdly. 'So you've come to an agreement with Biddulph?'

'I'll go ahead with or without you,' said James.

'You mentioned return cargoes. The Cape Verdes haven't enough feed to support a goat.'

'True. But they are within spitting distance of West Africa. Mahogany, copra, spices. The fruits of the earth.'

Cigar smoke drifted about the room in cobweb layers. The fire whispered dark secrets to itself. A French clock preserved time behind a glass cover. Silence imposed an unnatural stillness upon the three figures until a coal sputtered from the grate. Albert leaned forward, picked up the brass fire-tongues, and tossed it back into the gaping red maw.

Frazer wheezed an asthmatic sigh and looked across at his son. 'I'm too old a dog to learn new tricks, but it's your inheritance that will be at risk, Albert. The decision is yours.'

Albert hesitated while he tried to understand how he had managed to become ensnared yet again in one of James' tangled schemes.

'I'll put up twenty thousand,' he said.

His father bared yellow teeth in a grin of distaste. 'And mortgage your future into the bargain. You always were prodigal with other folk's money. Very well. I shall speak to Emma.' He held out a hand. 'I hope you know what you are doing, Onedin.'

'I know,' said James. He shook hands and steered Albert out of the office. Just give me the Cape Verdes, he thought, and the Brazil trade is mine.

Frazer turned his back on the closing door and gazed out through the window. Looking down upon the busy yards he watched a carpenter fashioning a spar with a lifetime's skill, the adze chipping and flaking until the surface was smooth as though planed. Others worked at caulking the deck planks of a slender-hulled ship, tamping in raw oakum and pouring in hot pitch from long-handled ladles. Riggers were securing new shrouds, leading the heavy four-stranded rope from the hounds down to the chain-plates and sweating them tight.

He turned his head to the left and followed an iron plate swinging high to the chunter of a steam crane. The plate was lowered and guided into position, and a swarm of riveters attacked it like demons, hammers swinging and pounding in a clamorous uproar that rang its challenge across the yard.

Frazer turned from the window and an unpleasant glimpse of a future in which he could play no part. The days of grace were over. The future lay in the hands of Albert and his kind.

CHAPTER THIRTEEN

The Azores stood out in the Atlantic a thousand miles west of Lisbon.

The *Barracuda* laboured against head winds and it was nine days before she threaded her way through the narrow channel separating Faial from the harsh rocky island of Pico to come to anchor in the tiny harbour of Horta.

Elizabeth, having gained the freedom of the ship, lolled contentedly, in a hammock strung between the awning rails on the poop and watched the land gliding past.

The air was hot and humid. Occasionally a flying-fish would flash like silver before plopping back into the still blue waters. A tiny town of many-hued houses clung precariously to the sides of a promontory stretching into the Atlantic like a bandaged thumb. A scattering of windmills gaily spun their sails above terraced fields hedged with vivid blue hydrangeas.

Across the channel the sea thundered against frozen streams of long-dead lava in great foam-spraying waves. Volcanic cliffs echoed to the cries of wandering frigate birds, and high above, the mist-enshrouded peak of Pico pointed to the skies.

The sun beat down from a dome of washed blue and Elizabeth, basking in oven heat, thought shipboard life the most languorous imaginable. She sipped lemonade and drowsed peacefully, the hammock rocking gently with the motion of the ship. From time to time she glanced at her arms, bare to the elbow and slowly turning to a delicate golden brown.

All her life she had been afraid of the deleterious effects of sunlight and had taken great care to shade her complexion from the glare of English summers, but now she had come to the conclusion that such fears were groundless, that in fact a syrupy-gold was most becoming. She held out her arm and, by turning it this way and that, could just see a faint fuzz of tiny hairs bleached almost white by the sun, and tried to imagine how she would look if browned all over. Only that morning she had stood unclothed in front of the mirror, and gazed at her reflection. The division between honey-brown and milky white gave her, she thought, an odd piebald appearance as though her form had been fashioned by some out-of-humour wayward sprite.

She had twisted and turned, viewing herself from all angles, until squinting through half-shuttered eyes, she had conjured the vision of a tawny, yellow-haired figure swaying voluptuously between the golden, cupid-adorned curlicues of the looking-glass and had wondered what effect it would have upon Daniel . . .

Daniel, she thought dreamily. His behaviour had been the very model of circumspection, civil in manner, obedient to her whims; and never once had he attempted to force his presence upon her. He had, thus far, shown evidence of a quite remarkable patience; most remarkable, given the circumstances and his notoriously short-fused temper.

On leaving Lisbon she had peremptorily demanded the key to her room and he had handed it over without demur. At first she had taken care to securely lock the door on entering or leaving, but as the heavy key, proved unwieldy to carry about during the day, she had simply made a point of locking herself in on retiring. Until last night. Last night she had deliberately left the door unlocked and, with a mixture of excitement and trepidation, had drawn the mosquito curtains and plunged beneath the thin coverlets. But nothing untoward had happened. No stealthy figure had slipped like a shadow into her room, and she had eventually fallen into a sound and dreamless sleep, lulled by the now-familiar run of water and the easy creak of the rigging, to awaken in the morning, relieved certainly, but also with just a trifle of disappointment.

She had dined and made friends with the two remaining officers, but quickly came to realize that for potential allies she must seek elsewhere. Mr Kennedy, the Mate, proved monosyllabic and hankered only for the day when he could return to his pudding wife and seven children. Mr Pawley, the second mate, gave her the creeps. He was a plump young man with a head like a rounded cheese, rubbery lips and a wet smile which seemed to dribble down his chin in rivulets of saliva. Both treated her with the deference due to the wife of a Master under God and continued to view her with the maddening tolerance shown to someone convalescing from a long and tiresome illness.

The sails were furled, a lighter came alongside, and the ship went about its business. Then suddenly Daniel was standing over her, his face crinkling into a smile.

'Would you like to go ashore?' he asked.

She swung from the hammock with alacrity and took his proffered arm. 'Oh, yes, indeed, Daniel,' she responded with the eagerness of a child offered a special treat and, hurrying below, changed into a light dress of frothy muslin and a pair of stout walking shoes.

On deck he greeted her with the delight of a schoolboy, guided her down the steep gangway ladder with its pipe-clayed handrails and concertina treads leading to a small platform awash with the hiss of the sea. A launch with a high curved prow, its stern covered with a fringed canopy waited alongside. A couple of bronzed islanders held the boat steady as Daniel stepped aboard, balanced easily and turned to hand her down. She took his hand, stepped upon one of the thwarts, lost her footing and stumbled against him. For a brief moment his arms encircled her and, as the boat rocked she took the opportunity to sway into his embrace. For a second or two they looked into each other's eyes, aware that the heaving of the boat was but the excuse each had been seeking. Then he guided her to the stern-sheets to sit beside her, as prim and proper as ever.

They landed at the side of a stone jetty and clambered up steps carved into rock and slippery with the wash of the sea. At the top they hobbled across ankle-wrenching cobbles which gave her another excuse to take Daniel's supporting arm while her memory, that traitor to the senses, took her back so many years to the little oil shop and Daniel's hand encompassing her breast.

The sun was a blaze of light, the streets steep and narrow, and it was only natural, therefore, that they should pause for refreshment at a small *taberna* buried in deep shade, where they drank a sweet local wine and ate dishes of tiny prawns grilled over charcoal while the proprietor fussed and bowed and spluttered at the honour done to his house. They idled their time, awkwardly shy with each other, then Daniel dug into his pocket and offered her a purse of sovereigns and a mixture of Portuguese money. 'I thought you might care to do a little shopping,' he said, adding apologetically as though holding himself to blame. 'I am afraid there are few goods of any quality. They sell mainly peasant wares.'

She was delighted, quickly finished her wine and hurried him off to bargain at stalls and tiny windowless shops painted vivid pinks and blues. She bought yards of coarse, brightly woven cloth, an immense straw hat, leather slippers and a wide leather waistband, half a dozen brilliantly-coloured skirts and blouses of fine lace. She bought everything in sight until Daniel, overloaded with packages, was forced to hire a couple of grinning urchins to carry her purchases back to the ship. Then he led her away before she could sack the town.

'Come along,' he said. 'There is much to see.'

Sitting astride a patient burro – and caring not a wit that she was exposing her limbs for all the world to see – she thought she had never known such a happy time.

England and Albert faded from memory and, as they climbed higher and higher along a narrow rubble-strewn track with the sea stretching far below like an ever-moving green-silk carpet, she thought it small wonder that men went to sea. Then, with many a side-long glance, she began to think seriously of a life spent with Daniel. If this was but a sample, then what other store of wonders could the future hold?

Dear Daniel, she thought. He really was such a romantic. To actually conceive of such a bold notion as kidnapping her. He had given up the world – just like Lord Hector in *Lord of the South Seas*. Lord Hector had spurned the hand of a high-born lady, renounced his title and eloped with a farmer's daughter to turn pirate and end his days as Rajah of some remote archipelego. Dear, dear Daniel. How could she possibly have thought ill of him?

Elizabeth looked with renewed interest and a lightening of the heart at the tall bearded figure lurching from side to side on the creaking saddle, his long legs almost touching the ground as his donkey, head bob-bobbing, plodded after their guide. Yes, all things considered, life with Daniel could be quite one long adventure.

They reached the peak and the breath caught in her throat. She felt as though she needed but to stretch out her arm and she could touch the snow-covered summit of Pico opposite. She looked down and for one dizzying moment had the sensation of falling. Then Daniel's arm steadied her as the high winds whipped at her skirts, tore the wide straw hat from her head and whirled it away to sail through the air like some strange yellow bird with outrageously rounded wings.

'Look,' said Daniel. 'Have you ever seen such a view?'

She raised her eyes and followed the sweep of his arm. It was like standing on the roof of the world. The Atlantic rolled away until it met the deeper blue of the sky. A giant's necklace of islands sprinkled the ocean, their colours varying from eye-aching blue to the green of jade. Each was surrounded by a froth of lace as the sea gnawed and worried at steep cliffs of black rock. Each bore above its head a cap of white cloud like a puff of pipe smoke. Each was rimmed and rounded at the top.

'Extinct volcanoes,' explained Daniel. He picked up a piece of porous rock as light as a feather. 'Well, almost extinct. The last erupted only twenty years ago.

Their guide, a bow-legged man with a warty face, tattered trousers and bare feet, spluttered something to Daniel. Daniel replied in the halting lingua franca of the sea, then took her by the hand.

'This way,' he said.

The guide trotted up a short steep grassy slope like a mountain goat while they slipped and slithered behind, their shod feet sliding on the tough wind-torn grass.

At the summit they stopped and the guide gestured with a proprietorial air.

Elizabeth bent her gaze and looked down into the mouth of hell.

'La Caldeira,' said the guide.

The crater was perfectly round and at the bottom nestled a lake out of a nightmare. Its surface boiled and gave off clouds of steam. Geysers spouted high into the air, died and roared again. The lake shore heaved and bubbled like a witches' cauldron. Evil pustules burst and threw off the foul stench of sulphur. Smoke billowed from black crevices and ice-cold waterfalls spurted from the crater's sides to meet the boiling lake in a hiss of spray and vapour. Fires glowed and rivers of molten lava flowed white hot before cooling to massive cinders which broke off to roll down to the waiting hell broth below.

Elizabeth shuddered and felt the ground tremble beneath her feet as a series of deep subterranean rumbles set the volcano into a paroxysm of coughing and spitting to spew fountains of boiling rock high into the air.

Daniel put an arm about her shoulders. 'It is quite safe,' he told her. 'The volcano is cooling. It won't erupt.' He smiled and gave her an affectionate squeeze. 'I would not permit it while you are here.'

She steeled herself to look once again. Down at the steaming jets rising from the thick boiling mire. Then she turned her head away, out to the cool, clean air and the vista of the endless sea, and wondered how such a paradise could exist at the very gates of Hell itself.

The guide led them back and halfway down they found a grassy plateau overlooking the sea and sheltered from the wind.

Daniel unpacked a hamper and they lunched off cold chicken, crusty fresh-baked bread, a bottle of wine, and finished with wild strawberries and fresh pineapples.

Replete at last she stretched out and sighed happily. She thought she had never, ever, known such a wonderful, wonderful day, and when Daniel leaned over and kissed her she thought she would swoon with sheer pleasure.

'Dear Daniel,' she murmured softly and would have liked to have said more but, conscious of the presence of the guide, contented herself with the gift of an encouraging smile.

He smiled in return then, swinging her to her feet, helped her to mount the burro who brayed indignation at being disturbed from its cropping of the lush green grass.

The tiny caravanserai wound its way back through ever-changing scenery, dropping down from the bleak mountain top with its sulphurous fumes and howling winds, to make its way through a natural hothouse where giant azaleas bloomed amid thickets of tree ferns and monkey trees stretched a lattice-work of skinny arms high above their heads.

The jungle vegetation ended abruptly at the edge of the town and, picking their way back to the quayside, they took the waiting boat to the ship.

Seated in the sternsheets, Elizabeth felt quite light-headed from the combined effects of wine, high altitude, and the memory of Daniel's kiss. She wondered how she could ever have doubted him. He was good, and kind, and honest, and she loved him passionately. Her mind drifted back through a golden haze to that secret time so long ago when they had loved so dearly and at such a cost in that raftered room with its blazing fire and oh-so-seductive divan.

The boat, bumping alongside the ship, brought her back to reality and, climbing the ladder swaying against the tarred shipside, she had a momentary sense of returning to prison.

Once in the privacy of her own room, however, she changed her opinion. A ship was a home. A refuge. An escape from the miseries of the world. On a ship problems were resolved by the simple expedient of hauling up the anchor and setting sail for exotic paradises where tomorrow was but another day. With dear Daniel it could, in truth, be an idyllic existence and she determined then and there to talk him out of this nonsense of becoming a sheep farmer. They would keep the ship and together drift from place to place as the will took them.

Unpacking her parcels and displaying the contents about the cabin, she sang softly to herself and thought it the most sensible idea she had ever had. She allowed her imagination to soar away on the wings of fancy until shadows crept across the room and the sun hid its disc behind the promontory and the sea flamed and ran like molten gold. The air was suddenly still, hot and humid, and Elizabeth discovered that she was developing a headache. Her temples throbbed, her eyes began to feel as though they were filled with sand, her mouth furred with the sticky aftermath taste of wine. She looked longingly at the bed and decided to take a nap before dinner.

Disrobing quickly, she slipped into her nightdress and then slid between the covers and luxuriated in the feathered embrace of the mattress. As her eyes closed she wondered drowsily if Daniel would come to her room. It would be exciting to awake and find him sleeping beside her. Then, unaccountably, she was sliding down a helter-skelter, travelling faster and faster until, with a soundless cry, she fell off the end to tumble down and down into the dark cavern of sleep. . . .

She awoke with a start, to find her heart thumping madly and with the firm conviction that the ship was on fire. She sat up quickly. The open portholes were wide round eyes peering into the total darkness of the cabin. The ship was as silent as a tomb. She widened her eyes, straining to pierce the gloom, then was almost blinded by a searing white flash that momentarily lit the room with a harsh brilliance before plunging it into an even deeper blackness. The flash was followed by a long, low rumbling, increasing in tempo until it exploded overhead with a crack that threatened to shake the ship to pieces.

Dragging her confused mind from the depths of sleep, she became convinced that the island had erupted to bury the town under a mountain of ash and that only she was left alive. Then as flash succeeded flash and the accompanying noise rose to a crescendo, she realized with a flood of relief that it was nothing other than a thunderstorm.

Even as a child, Elizabeth had been attracted to the occasional angry tempests which roared and rolled across the heavens, and would stand for hours staring in mesmeric fascination at the play of lightning, longing for – and sometimes blasphemously praying for – a sight of it striking and destroying. But it had never happened. The storm had invariably passed overhead, and the following day the newspapers would be filled with reports of haystacks set afire, cows charred to cinders, of miraculous escapes of old folks sitting by their chimney-pieces. She had never known the slightest apprehension, although young Robert had trembled and quaked like a jelly with his head buried beneath the blankets.

She rose quickly and, hurrying to the nearest porthole, peered out across the harbour.

Never having witnessed a tropic storm before, she was quite unprepared for the explosion of violence which met her gaze. Thunder roared from a black sky while the massive shoulder of Pico bellowed back defiance. Lightning tore the sky apart, flared from Pico's glistening flanks, then hissed overhead with the sound of tearing silk. The sea lay like a black mirror reflecting the burning heavens above. Brilliant incandescence alternated with the totality of pitch-darkness. Far-distant islands, like lonely outposts, shouted their challenge, and mountains and gorges echoed and re-echoed their anger.

Elizabeth craned her neck but Pico was too close. She longed to see that lofty, snow-covered peak defying the challenge of the gods. It was common knowledge that the higher an object the more the likelihood of its being struck. As Pico rose almost 8,000 feet from the sea, far higher than any chimney stack she could ever remember seeing, this seemed an excellent opportunity to view the effect of a thunderbolt.

She turned away, hurriedly put on her light cotton nightgown, and pattered up on to deck.

Emerging into the open air, she found the great bowl of the sky riven by jagged flashes. Lightning danced and flickered about the mountain peaks while thunder rolled and crashed until the very earth seemed to shake. As she watched, breathless with excitement, a clump of trees on the opposite shore suddenly burst into flames to send showers of sparks flying into the air like swarms of fireflies. She gaped in wonder, then suddenly Daniel was standing beside her.

He had divested himself of his jacket and his white shirt and white duck trousers gave him the spectral appearance of an apparition conjured by the gods of the sea.

He mistook her startled gasp and stretched out a comforting arm. Then he, too, jumped, as her nightgown crackled and a tiny blue spark leapt the gap between them. He laughed nervously. 'There is nothing to be afraid of,' he assured her, 'It is no more than a manifestation of atmospheric electricity. Quite a common phenomenon in tropic climes.' He waved an arm. 'You see the entire crew are sleeping through it quite undisturbed.'

'But I am not afraid,' she protested, then frowned. 'Asleep? What time is it?'

'Approaching six bells – about three o'clock in the morning.' He smiled and an aureole of light played behind his beaded head. 'You must have slept like a log. I did look in to call you for dinner, but you were snoring like a little fat porker.'

'I am not fat, and I don't snore,' she retorted indignantly.

Daniel grinned impertinently. 'You were shaking the rafters.'

A burst of lightning, ripping apart the sky, seemed to scorch the very air and then, quite without warning, a storm of hailstones beat down with savage ferocity, drumming on the decks and lashing through her thin night attire like a thousand whips. She shivered and whimpered and buried her head in his chest as he put comforting arms about her. Then, just as suddenly, the hail turned to rain. An icy downpour that drenched them to the skin, while the lightning flared and turned the rain into curtains of white fire. She felt his warmth and huddled closer. Then, raising her head as his hands slid selectively down, she pushed into him, leaned back her head and opened her mouth. The thunder roared about her ears and the lightning turned his face into a blur of light as his mouth found hers. The world turned, then he drew away as the sky emptied of rain, scooped her up in his arms, and carried her below.

Daniel deposited her in her room and stood, arms akimbo, grinning down at her. She brushed a wet tangle of hair from her face and shivered at the clammy touch of thin cotton while the room blazed and blazed again in a tempest of light.

He stood hesitating as though expecting dismissal, water

streaming from his sodden clothes and forming a pool about his feet.

'Don't go, Daniel,' she said.

He squelched towards her and they met to cling together like two wet sponges. He drew back to survey her ruefully. 'You'd better dry off before you catch pneumonia.' He grinned. 'I don't want to lose you now.'

'Don't go,' she pleaded, alarmed that she might be left alone forever.

'I'll be back in a few moments,' he promised, sneezed explosively, and disappeared into the dark cavern of the alleyway beyond.

She quickly peeled off her night attire and, teeth chattering, towelled herself dry, hastily dragged brush and comb through her hair, and then plunged into bed to lie a-tremble while the drum-roll of thunder drifted away and the flare of lightning lost its harshness to flicker pink and ghostly blue.

Daniel seemed to be taking an unconscionable time and she subjected herself to the tormenting picture of him hurrying towards her then being struck by lightning like Jack Merriman in *The Prodigal's Return*. Surely fate could not be so cruel? Then an image of Albert's calm good-humoured face rose like a spectre from the past, only to be banished immediately to the limbo from which it had sprung. After all, she argued crossly, had Albert not betrayed her with that ridiculous painted hussy from a flower shop? – or a sewer, for aught she knew or cared. And how many other raddled creatures had there been? Furthermore, had she not sworn a lasting oath to revenge herself? And what sweeter revenge than this? Glowing with self-justification, Elizabeth drew down the top sheet to display her elegancies to the best advantage, then, re-arranging her hair to fall about her shoulders in ordered disarray, clasped her hands behind her head, closed her eyes, and waited for Daniel.

When she opened them again Daniel was standing sheepishly in the doorway. He wore a new brocaded dressing-gown reeking of mothballs and carried a bottle of wine.

'I am afraid we have no champagne this time,' he smiled, padding across the room.

She understood his reference. 'This time it will be much, much better,' she promised, holding out her arms.

He perched on the edge of the bed, drew back the top cover and kissed each soft welcoming mound while she sighed and purred in blissful rapture. Then, tugging aside the sheet, she wriggled invitingly to one side, while he fumbled clumsily with the stiff fastenings of his dressing-gown and the lightning filled the room with its uneathly glow and tears of rain streamed down the glass ports.

Then he was beside her, his hands running over her body like fire. Mouth found mouth and they interlaced in a wild tangle of limbs. He was about to roll on top of her but she stayed him and, with an insistent pressure of her fingers, pushed him over on to his back.

'Wait,' she whispered softly. 'Wait. Now it is my turn.' She rose above him. 'Lie still, my sweet. There, there, my beauty.' She plunged down, impaling herself upon the waiting spear of flesh. 'There, there,' she said, crooning and leaning forward. 'There, my pet, my beauty, my love.' As his hands sought and found her breasts she rose and fell, rose and fell, tormenting him until his face twisted in anguish and at last they reached a mindless ecstasy which left them bereft of sense, or form, or time, and she knew that she could never, never leave him.

Later they lay side by side and, dizzily content, watched the glow of dawn slowly fill the room with roseate light.

She nestled in the crook of his arm. 'Oh, Daniel,' she murmured. 'I do love you so.'

He stretched lazily. 'We shall cruise the islands,' he promised. 'It will be our honeymoon. We have plenty of time. All the time in the world.'

CHAPTER FOURTEEN

A day out from Liverpool the *Firefly*, braced hard on the port tack, swept out into the Atlantic, spray bursting over her bows, her lee rail almost under.

James, his back against the weather rail, watched Albert

taking pot shots at chips of wood tossed over the side by the ship's apprentice, a spotty-faced child wearing a cloth cap falling about his ears and an oversize suit of reach-me-downs.

'Throw.'

Albert held the pistol at arm's length, squinted along the sights and pulled the trigger.

The bullet skittered across the top of a wave, a yard from the target. 'Missed again,' said Albert. He re-loaded, shifted his stance and held the weapon upright like a duellist.

'Throw.'

He straightened his arm, the gun boomed, seabirds wheeled and called derisively as the shot fell wide.

'I shouldn't worry,' said James sardonically. 'Daniel Fogarty will present a much larger target and no doubt be gentleman enough to stand still.'

'Throw,' called Albert, took aim and tightened his finger. The chip of wood fractured into splinters. 'A hit!' crowed the apprentice. 'A bull's-eye!'

'Throw.'

James, bored with the game, climbed the poop ladder and joined Baines. The giant shook his massive head. 'I don't like it. He's going to get himself killed.'

'He will if he comes within arm's length,' James agreed. 'Daniel Fogarty will simply break his back and pitch him over the side.'

Baines removed his cap and scratched his head. 'Then what do we do?'

'Keep 'em apart,' said James. 'I'll deal with Fogarty.'

The gun banged again.

'Close,' said Baines. He walked to the lee rail, ejected a stream of tobacco juice and returned. 'It's a cold-blooded way o' fighting.'

'It's a gentleman's way,' said James. 'They fight to kill.'

Baines bit off another enormous chaw of tobacco, chewed reflectively, then wedged it into the side of his cheek. 'It would be murder,' he complained. 'Daniel Fogarty couldn't hit a barn door if he had hold of the handle. In any case, where would he put his hands on a gun the match of that?'

'Albert's brought a pair. One each.'

Baines snorted, slewed the wodge of tobacco in his cheek. 'He seems to have thought of everything.'

The gun banged and splinters of wood flew into the air.

'Pray God we never catch up with him,' said Baines piously.

'You'd better pray we do,' James told him tartly. 'Otherwise you may find yourself seeking another command.' He walked away, paused at the head of the ladderway and glanced up at the set of the sails. 'Since when have we been flying Irish pennants, Captain Baines?' he demanded irritably, and pointed to the end of the foremast lower yard where an offending piece of rope yarn streamed in the wind. 'Attend to it, if you please.'

'Aye, aye,' growled Baines, affronted. In all probability the strands of yarn had been whisked aloft by the wind and become trapped in the sheaf of the brace block. It was unlikely to have been left by a careless seaman. Not on any ship that Baines commanded. Nevertheless Irish pennants were a sure indication of a slovenly crew and, by implication, of slack discipline.

Baines cast an eye around. 'Mr Norman!' he bawled.

The apprentice jumped a yard into the air and dropped his armful of chippings. 'Sus-sus sir?'

'Aloft with ye,' roared Baines. 'Free that bloody yarn! Have ye no eyes in your head, young man?'

Mr Norman, all of thirteen years and making his first voyage, followed the direction of his captain's gaze, gulped, scrambled into the weather shrouds and gingerly clambered aloft.

'Keep her steady,' Baines warned the helmsman. 'He's naught but a little lad.'

It wasn't much of a climb, as climbs go aboard a full-rigged ship, but it was enough to turn Mr Norman's face a pasty green.

Albert paused at his target practice. James watched from the shelter of the overhanging poop deck. The job watch turned grinning faces upward.

Whether it was consciousness of the concentration of stares, or a momentary dizziness, or just plain fear that caused it, but inching his way along the yard, foot by tremulous foot, the lower topmast sail booming above his head and the lower course thrumming at his feet, young Mr Norman suddenly lost his grip and, with a despairing yell, pitched from the yard, hit the shrouds and bounced off into the racing sea.

He came to the surface as the ship flew past in a welter of foam. Albert kicked off his shoes, dragged his arms free of his jacket and went over the side in a flailing dive to hit the water with a force that knocked the breath from his body and tumbled him over and over like a rag doll. He came to the surface, choking for air and a pain knifing through his chest, to discover the ship a quarter of a mile away and a cloth cap bobbing beside him. He trod water, gulped air, and a wave hoisting him to its crest allowed a glimpse of a spotty face and a pair of wildly floundering arms a couple of hundred yards distant. The head disappeared into the trough of a succeeding wave as Albert struck out towards the youth's despairing wail.

Swimming for your life in the Atlantic, he soon found, was vastly different from splashing about off New Brighton beach. Atlantic rollers measured a hundred feet from crest to crest while the troughs were plunging roils of water twenty feet deep. Albert raised his head at the top of the next wave and realized that he was lost in a wilderness of ocean.

Aboard ship James seized a lifebelt and, bawling, 'Man overboard!' hurled it over the side. The helmsman put the helm down bringing the ship's head up into the wind. Baines took up James' cry and roared out commands to a crew already scurrying to their stations.

The watch below tumbled out on to deck, raced to sheets and braces, while the boat's crew cleared away the quarter boat. They were already lowering away as the *Firefly* spun on her heels and, with sails backed, drifted down towards Albert's bobbing head. Of young Mr Norman there was no sign.

Albert coughed up a mouthful of stomach-retching salt water, saw a pair of trouser bottoms ballooning to the surface, grabbed the leather belt, heaved, and went under.

A pair of legs kicked feebly. Albert grasped a collar and a round puffy face rose from the sea, panic-stricken eyes glassy with terror, then a pair of arms wrapped about his neck and they submerged together like lovers locked in an eternal embrace. They broke the surface in the trough of a wave and Albert savagely butted the face in front of him, broke free of the strangling grip, dived and came up behind the boy. He gripped him by the shoulders and leaned back kicking out strongly in the manner recommeneded by his swimming instructor. Then the mountain of water curling above their heads broke into a smother of foam, while the powerful undertow pulled them apart like two rag dolls.

Something thumped Albert on the head. Turning, he saw a circular red and white lifebelt slithering down the moiling cliff of water. He reached out despairingly, clutched one of the lifelines lopped about it, pulled it towards him and hung on to the buoyant cork, his head spinning dizzily, stomach heaving and the breath labouring in his chest. He had been in the sea for no more than three minutes and already he felt like a half-drowned rat, the enormous depths pulling at his feet while the lifebelt, spinning slowly, rising and falling, became a tiny island refuge in the limitless expanse of the ocean.

Then a voice hailed him and the stern of the ship's boat lifted high from the trough of the next wave. Willing hands reached out and dragged him to safety. He lay on the bottom boards struggling weakly like a newly-landed fish and saw James' face grinning down at him.

'The boy?' he gasped through a throat that burned like fire.

James uncorked a flask. 'Drink this,' he said.

The brandy scorched its way down to his stomach and Albert coughed and retched again as one of the seaman bawled: 'I see un. Paddle yer hands, young shaver. Paddle yer hands.'

Albert sat up in time to see the bedraggled Mr Norman hauled over the side more dead than alive and tumbled into the bottom of the boat. Then the cold bit into him, his limbs seemed turned to ice, his teeth rattled and chattered in his head, and he shook and shivered uncontrollably from head to foot.

James forced the neck of the flask between his teeth. 'Get it down,' he commanded. 'All you can swallow.'

Albert gulped obediently and then floated away on a sea of darkness.

When he next opened his eyes it was to find himself lying in his bunk, cocooned in blankets and muzzy with the effects of brandy. He focused his eyes and found James looking down at him quizzically.

'How – how is the lad?' he managed to croak.

'Sitting up and taking nourishment, and none the worse for

his ducking. He's the darling of the ship and enjoying every moment of it. As for you, young Albert, kindly remember in future that you are a passenger and leave the heroics to those who are paid for it. The sole consequence of your efforts was to give us two people to rescue instead of one. Now lie still. I don't think you have broken anything, but there is something odd. Very odd.'

'Broken—?' Albert remembered the smash of water and the knifing pain in his chest. Concurrent with the memory came another – of his ribs splintering and caving in under the impact of a flailing arm of metal.

James' fingers were exploring the sides of his rib cage. 'Diving overboard from a ship under way can have much the same effect as jumping from a moving train. Now breathe deeply and steadily.'

Albert obediently drew in a breath and blew it out again.

James stood up and scratched his head. 'I have a notion you have lost the use of one of your lungs. I shouldn't worry,' he added cheerfully. 'You'll be a mite short of breath for the rest of your life, but you'll live long enough to plague us all.'

'Lost a lung . . .?' Albert blinked in disbelief and searched his chest as though expecting to find the missing article lying beside him.

'Punctured,' James corrected. 'At least that is my guess. I think perhaps we should put you ashore at our next port of call.'

'No,' said Albert firmly. 'No hospitals.' Like many of his generation Albert had a morbid and abiding horror of such institutions, and an even greater horror of the operating table.

'As you wish,' James agreed, sharing the same animus. 'But if the mountain won't go to Mohammed, then we must needs fetch Mohammed to the mountain. You will submit to being examined by the port medical authority and abide by his decision.'

Albert opened his mouth in protest.

'If you don't,' said James levelly. 'Baines will be constrained to put you ashore as unfit to travel.'

'You wouldn't dare,' said Albert weakly, and looking into those bleak eyes, knew that James would.

James rubbed his hands. 'In the meantime, take your medicine like a man.' He held out a glass of foul-tasting liquid. 'Swallow it down.'

Albert gagged and pulled a wry face as his tongue seemed to cleave to the roof of his mouth. 'What on earth is it?' he managed at last.

'One of Baines' favourite specifics,' James told him. He hauled the blankets up to Albert's chin. 'A mixture of brandy, laudanum, oil of peppermint and a few cloves to give it body. You'll sleep like a babe and wake like a lion.'

He blew out the light and even as the door closed behind him, Albert's snores reverberated throughout the cabin.

While the *Barracuda* drifted through idyllic days and the *Firefly* tore across the ocean, Sarah, taking the opportunity of practising chapter two of *The Perfect Hostess*, was engaged in entertaining an ill-tempered Mr Biddulph, a calm Cousin Richard, and a demure Leonora, to tea.

The young people had been constant visitors of late and, in truth, seemed to use the Croxteth Road address as a trysting place. They were rarely out of each other's company and Leonora had endeared herself to Sarah's heart by constantly commenting in the most *favourable* terms on Sarah's exquisite taste in her employment of the accoutrements of the home, while Cousin Richard for his part would listen for hours agreeing wholeheartedly with Robert's pontifications. 'Why,' he had once pronounced admiringly, after a long, interminable peroration. 'You should be in Parliament.'

Sarah could sense which way the wind was blowing. and if it were not for the fear of that crotchety Mr Biddulph withdrawing his support from dear Robert, she would have wished the couple well and employed every artifice to ensure they made a match of it – even were it only to put James' nose out of joint. But that crab-faced old monster nibbling at her cucumber sandwiches was certainly not a man to be trifled with.

He had descended upon them choking with choler, brushed aside the maid and marched into the drawing-room like a prophet of doom.

Sarah, armed with only two chapters of *The Perfect Hostess*, and wishing she had read further, greeted him with the civility which protocol demanded, seated him in a chair, fed him sandwiches for which he seemed to have a voracious appetite, the while devoting herself to the practice of the Art of Conversation recommended in chapter one.

It soon became painfully apparent, however, that Mr Biddulph was quite unfamiliar with the works of the anonymous Lady of Quality responsible for the instruction of lesser mortals in the ways of Society. Biddulph simply munched his sandwiches, guzzled his tea and fixed a basilisk stare upon the pair of innocents seated opposite.

The conversation trickled away into a pool of silence. Sarah flipped open her fan, fluttered the air, and remarked upon the inclemency of the weather.

Biddulph snorted, put down cup and saucer with a clatter, and addressed himself directly to Cousin Richard.

'What the devil do you mean by it, sir! I have heard rumours, sir, rumours!'

Sarah picked up the cup and saucer. 'You will take another dish of tea?' she asked politely, remembering that *as guests may be embarrassed by requesting a second serving, the considerate hostess will not at first take 'no' for an answer,* refilled the cup.

'Rumours?' asked Richard easily. 'I believe I misunderstand you, sir.'

'Sugar?' questioned Sarah. 'One lump, or two?'

'Two!' snapped Biddulph, and returned his attention to Richard. 'I must ask you, sir, to declare your intentions towards my daughter.'

'My intentions,' Richard returned coldly. 'Are by no means as unworthy as your suspicions. Miss Leonora has been gracious enough to honour me with her company . . .'

'There is gossip, sir, gossip.'

'To which, I trust, you pay no attention.'

'Do try some of this excellent seed cake,' urged Sarah. 'It is from a very old recipe and I would so much appreciate your opinion.'

'Damn you and your seed cake!' roared Biddulph. 'As for you, Mr Onedin, it should be needless to remind you that my daughter is utterly lacking in guile, and cannot therefore be expected to comprehend the wiles and stratagems of idle-tongued rumour-mongers, but you and I, sir, are men of the world and can fully appreciate the damage to which such traducers can commit a young girl's reputation. Dammit, sir, the child is never free of your company!'

'Ginger cake?' asked Sarah, persuasively.

Biddulph absently took a piece of the proffered cake, stared at it as though it had done him an injury, and returned it to the plate. 'Furthermore, young man, you cannot but be aware that Leonora is betrothed to Mr Onedin.'

'Subject to contract, as I understand it,' said Richard coolly.

'I beg your pardon?'

'No matter.' Richard stifled a yawn and turned his attention to Sarah. 'Prior to Mr Biddulph honouring us with his presence, I was about to remark that I am now prepared to underwrite cousin Robert's business commitments, and that I have also availed myself of the privilege of putting his name forward as a prospective candidate in the Liberal interests. I am sure that cousin Robert could be quite an ornament to the Council.'

The gentle irony was lost upon Sarah who quivered like a female Moses vouchsafed a glimpse of the Promised Land.

'It is the least we can do,' said Leonora, openly taking Richard's hand and giving it a fond squeeze.

'In return for your hospitality,' added Richard. 'No more than a small earnest of my appreciation.'

Biddulph had an uneasy sense that the ground was being cut from beneath his feet. This pale-faced, carrot-headed young man was far too confident.

'I think,' he said testily. 'We should keep to the point.'

Sarah tried to pour a little oil on troubled waters. 'Do allow me to assure you, dear Mr Biddulph, that these two young people have always conducted themselves with the greatest propriety.'

'Am I then to understand, madam, that you have been party to this deception?' Biddulph demanded irascibly.

Sarah bridled. 'Really, sir, you go too far!' With the carrot of the town council dangling appetizingly within reach she quickly changed allegiances. 'Your presence is no longer welcome in this house.'

Biddulph hauled himself to his feet. 'Very well, madam, then there is no more to be said. I bid you good-day. Come, Leonora.'

Leonora shook chestnut ringlets. 'No, Papa.'

'What!' Biddulph's features took on a mottled hue. 'You dare to defy me, Miss?'

'I am sorry, Papa, but I have quite changed my mind and no longer have the inclination to marry James. It is dear Richard to whom I have promised my heart.' The brown eyes gazed guilessly at her father while their possessor waited for her beloved to deliver the *coup de grace.*

'You have – quite changed – your mind?' Biddulph could not believe the evidence of his ears. 'Allow me to remind you, Miss Pick-and-Choose, that you are not yet of an age to possess a mind to change.' He rounded on Richard. 'As for you, sir, I forbid you to continue this association for one moment longer.'

'A pity,' said Richard. 'We were hoping for your blessing.'

'You will require more than my blessing,' Biddulph told him icily. 'Leonora has not yet reached the age of consent.'

Richard shrugged. 'If you intend to play the tyrant, I am afraid you leave me little option.'

'Option!' snarled Biddulph. 'You have no option. Leonora will marry James Onedin. You have my word on it.'

'From what I know of Cousin James,' said Richard calmly. 'I doubt he will relish the prospect of marrying into a bankrupt family.'

'What—'

'You have been extending your interests. Opening up a new coalfield, I understand? To which end you have borrowed substantially.'

'With ample security.'

Richard shook his head. His manner hardened and he stared at the older man with eyes as cold and bleak as James.' 'Not ample enough. I hold your paper.'

There was a prolonged silence broken by the rattle of a cup and saucer.

'More tea?' asked Sarah brightly.

Elizabeth shuttered her eyes against the fierce rays of the

Jamaican sun and peered through blood-red curtains into the dream-world of the past few weeks . . .

They had drifted through amethyst seas where islands rose like green jewels and giant suns set against lilac skies. They had visited each of the islands in turn, from St Miguel with its twin lakes set in sylvan glades, to Flores in the far west, off whose shores Richard Grenville's *Revenge* had fought its last bloody battle.

As day followed golden day they had loved, tumbling into sleep, to awaken and love again, each teaching and learning from the other. She thought she had never known such rapture, and even after those enchanted isles had dropped beyond the horizon and the ship had lost itself in the vast eternity of the sea, they had continued to despoil each other to the song of the wind in the rigging and the chuckle of water running beneath the counter, until overcome with satiety they drowsed side by side and planned for an idyllic future in which day to day problems played no part.

But within the week they had sighted Cuba, taken the Windward Passage, and picked up the green turtle-backed island of Jamaica, while the deep blue water turned pale green and the high peaks of the Blue Mountains, clothed in violet shadows, loomed against the sky.

The *Barracuda* had sounded its way through the shoals and finally dropped anchor in Spanish Town's tiny harbour.

They had gone ashore together, boldly as man and wife, and wandered through market stalls piled with fruit.

Stalks of green and yellow bananas snuggled close to pyramids of golden oranges, coconuts rubbed hairy shoulders with bundles of sugar cane, while blackamoors in coloured kerchiefs and with water-melon grins shouted their wares in a patois of Creole and Elizabethan English.

Elizabeth had thought she had never known such a happy people and, wanting to share her own private happiness with them, had bought and bought again until Daniel, loaded to the chin, had laughingly led her away to walk through narrow streets of tumbledown shops and peeling houses that meandered back from the jetty.

Daniel had seemed to know his way and she had followed

dutifully, imagining that he was about to reveal some further wonder of this wondrous voyage. A narrow doorway leaned back from the glare of the street, and he had stepped aside to usher her inside, when a sun-blistered sign had caught her eye and sent her heart plummeting like a leaden weight.

CALLON & Co.

it read, and she had a momentary picture of long octopus tentacles reaching out across the world to pluck them from paradise.

'Come along,' Daniel had called cheerfully, depositing his mound of purchases into the arms of a porter who lurched on a peg leg from the darkness beyond. 'It is only our office. A few minutes' business to conduct and then we shall be free again.'

Free? she had thought miserably. Would they ever be free? Could not Daniel realize that they were now pariahs? Outcasts? They would never be free. Albert would hunt them down. And even if he should fail society would turn its back on them. There could be no returning.

She had followed him up a flight of rickety stairs and sat in a cane-backed chair in an office smelling of must, with jewel-eyed lizards motionless on the walls, while Daniel arranged for the discharge of cargo with a fat perspiring man in a shabby suit of shantung. He and Daniel had finally exchanged civilities, pledged each other with glasses of fiery rum, and the fat man had remarked that a Callon ship had been spoken off the Point. The *Firefly*, he understood from her signal letters. No doubt Captain and the charming Mrs Fogarty would wish to go aboard and pay their compliments? All, he had assured them with a flap of hands like pudgy white butterflies, would be arranged. . . .

Elizabeth sat up and opened her eyes. For a few moments, as her vision readjusted itself, the sky turned purple and the tough sword grass bowed and waved in an ancient dance to the thin piping of the sea breeze.

Looking down she saw, far below, a toy harbour with toy ships and a cluster of toy houses. A tiny ship with outspread wings like a white bird was rounding the headland and picking its way though the milky-white shoal water. It must be the

Firefly she thought, and rose to her feet with a sense of foreboding. Outward bound from England it would almost certainly carry news of her escapade. On leaving the agent's office they had agreed that Elizabeth should remain ashore while Daniel dealt with the master of the *Firefly*. She had agreed to wait until the *Barracuda* flew the affirmative flag C, and then make her way back to the ship. Tomorrow, cargo or no cargo, they would sail.

Plans, she thought, always plans. Was this, then, to be their life. Planning and running, planning and running?

She made her way slowly down the winding, twisting path that rambled down the side of the hill as though it had nowhere to go, and realized with sick despair that Daniel would never outface a problem, would always take the easy way and run. For all his seeming strength he had the weakness of a child afraid of what tomorrow might bring. He needed her. Albert, and James, and even Robert in his own way, were self-sufficient, but Daniel, dear Daniel, preferred to be led by the nose. He had moved up in the world because he had been pliant to Callon's will. He had married Emma because it had been the line of least resistance. And even her own abduction had not been the action of a man of decision. He had left all to chance. And now new fears had him by the throat. For what had he said but, 'go away and hide and I will pretend it never happened?' when all she wanted was for them to stand together and face the world.

Moodily she trudged aboard the *Barracuda* and made her way below. Peering through a port, she watched the *Firefly* coming to anchor.

The ship came in close-hauled, squared her yards, smartly clewed up fore and main topsails, hauled down her jib and streamed the anchor buoy. The anchor left the cat-head and hit the water with a splash. Even as she payed out cable the ship's boat swung out, cast off and made for the *Barracuda*.

There was something familiar about the figure sitting upright in the stern-sheets. James! Her heart leapt into her mouth. James! Was there to be no escape . . .?

She left her vantage point and paced restlessly about the room then, hurrying to her trunkful of purchases quickly rummaged through the contents. So be it! She would give her brother something to gossip about when he returned home . . .

James stepped briskly aboard the *Barracuda,* caught Fogarty's startled eye, and bared his teeth in greeting.

Daniel stared at the apparition in utter disbelief. 'Onedin! What the devil brings you here?'

'Elizabeth,' said James without formality. 'I've come to take her home.'

'You'll be out of luck,' said Daniel, recovering his wits. He jerked his head. 'You'd better come below.'

James' eyes narrowed as he followed. The man seemed unexpectedly sure of himself and there was an uncommonly jaunty look about the set of his shoulders as he led the way along the deck.

Fogarty stepped aside as they entered the saloon. James halted on the threshold as an Elizabeth he had never known rose coolly to extend a brown hand in welcome.

'Why, James!' she exclaimed. 'What a delightful surprise.'

Her blue eyes looked artlessly from a nutmeg brown face. A pony tail of hair hung down her back. She wore a bright red peasant blouse and trousers of white kid held to a slender waist by a broad belt of soft leather with an enormous silver buckle. A barbaric gold ring with an immense green emerald glowed on her extended left hand. She held a cigar between her teeth, and blew out a cloud of fragrant smoke.

'How good of you to call,' she cooed. She moved across and linked her arm to Daniel's. 'You really must stay to dinner and tell us *all* the news. Mustn't he, Daniel?'

'Of course,' said Daniel, almost as dazed as James.

James sniffed, looked from one to the other. 'So that's the way of it? It won't do, Elizabeth. It won't do at all. I have come to fetch you home.'

She gave him a flash of white teeth and gestured with her free arm. 'But *this* is our home, James. And I am quite content.'

'But Albert isn't,' said James. 'He needs you.'

'But I don't need him,' said Elizabeth. 'Do convey my apologies . . .'

James brusquely cut her short. 'You don't understand. Albert is aboard the *Firefly*. He is a sick man. If you want my opinion I doubt he will survive the voyage home.'

She stared at him. It was unfair. So grossly unfair. 'I am sorry,' she said. 'But I am not going back.'

'You are,' said James. 'Or I will leave you both penniless on the beach.'

Daniel was the first to find his tongue. 'You will what . . .?'

James fished a document from his pocket. 'Read that,' he said curtly.

Elizabeth looked over Daniel's shoulder at the neat copperplate writing. 'What is it?' she asked anxiously.

Daniel frowned. 'A bill of sale . . .?'

'For ship and cargo,' said James.

Daniel shook his head, 'It's not worth the paper it's written on. It's dated. . . .'

'It is dated after you left everything to Emma. You never did have a head for business, Fogarty. You renounced your holdings before taking the *Barracuda*.'

Daniel thrust the paper back at him. 'A lawyer's quibble.'

'Lawyers' quibbles make law,' said James. 'And that document is perfectly legal. I have it on the best authority.'

'Damn you and your authority. We are not in England.'

'No,' said James. 'But we are in British territory.' He waited for the import to sink in. 'The choice is yours. Elizabeth. Or ship and cargo.'

Elizabeth stared at Daniel and read the indecision in his face.

'No!' she screamed. 'No!'

'Be quiet, madam,' snapped James 'You have already cost me a deal of money and time I can ill afford.'

'Money!' she screeched. 'Money! Am I for sale!'

'I don't know,' said James coldly. 'Shall we find out?'

Daniel slowly paced the cabin. 'If that document is valid. . . .'

'You'll starve together,' said James.

'Daniel . . .!' Elizabeth called to him across an ever-widening distance. 'Daniel! Please! We shall manage. You can find work.'

'Not here,' said Daniel. 'I have seen men wasted and broken. And women . . . No – I could not subject you to that.'

'Daniel . . .!' she wailed.

Daniel avoided her eyes and looked at James. 'I'll take the ship. But mark me, Onedin – I'll be back. And when I do, guard your gates.'

'Ships!' she screamed at them. 'Ships! That is all you ever think of! Ships, ships, ships!' She sat down, knowing she had lost and, cupping her face in her hands, sobbed and sobbed until she thought her heart would break.

'I'll wait for you aboard the *Firefly*,' said James, turned on his heel and left them alone.

Elizabeth, stiff-faced and hollow-eyed, was swung aboard the *Firefly* in a basket chair. She brought no baggage, no effects, and wore the same hooped crinoline, the same embroidered jacket she had worn when leaving Liverpool a world of time ago. Scorning James' proffered hand she made her own way below to Albert's cabin.

He lay wasted and feverish, sweating and shivering, his eyes bright with delirium. She took one of the thin hot hands and stroked it gently. 'Poor Albert,' she whispered. 'Poor, poor Albert,' and fresh tears began to course down her cheeks.

He ran his tongue over lips caked with dried spittle, and focused his eyes.

'Elizabeth?' His voice was a whisper no louder than the dry rustle of leaves.

'Dear Albert,' she said.

He summoned up a vestige of his old mocking smile. 'I'm in damnable shape. Must have caught a chill. You should have brought your bold captain – I might have been able to pass it on.'

She smiled through her tears. 'It will be all right, Albert. I am coming home.'

'Did . . .?'

She shook her head, understanding the question. 'No, Albert,' she lied. 'I led him a dog's life. He was ready to pack me off home when James arrived.'

He squeezed her hand. 'James said that he would have caught a Tartar.' His eyes closed and he began to shake and shiver violently while strange croakings emerged from his throat.

She released his hand and walked to James watching from the doorway. 'What is it?'

'Blood poisoning,' said James.

'How...?'

James shrugged. 'I don't know. It commenced a few days ago. He's going fast, Elizabeth.'

Elizabeth stayed with him until the end, eating little and sleeping less. She offered what comfort she could, and he rallied once or twice.

'We must thank James,' he said once. 'Without him I would never have found you. He has a sharp brain, your brother. Sharpest chap I ever met. Told him so, once. Long time ago. I remember how he put a spoke in Fogarty's wheel. Much to thank him for. Much.'

She remembered and filed the information away. One day there would be a reckoning and brother James would live to regret the day he was born.

Four days later Albert closed his eyes for the last time and his body grew cold. They laid him to rest in the Sargasso Sea while Baines intoned: 'We therefore commit his body to the deep, to be turned into corruption, looking for the resurrection of the body, when the sea shall give up her dead....'

A bubble gulped from the sea, then the brown Sargasso weed entwined long arms in benediction over the ring of water and closed the monstrous depths below.

Baines shut the prayer book with a snap and nodded to the Mate. 'All hands make sail, if you please, Mr Armstrong.'

It was not perhaps a fitting epitaph for a man who had spent his life dreaming of steamships, but there was nothing left to be said.

Elizabeth stood alone at the stern and looked back, out to the far horizon, across the great heaving mat of weed parting and then closing behind the ship's wake, out beyond the horizon, out to enchanted isles and enchanted days, out to a ship winging south like a white bird and carrying dear, foolish, weak Daniel out of her life forever.

A figure appeared at her side. 'I'm sorry,' said James. 'You will miss him.'

She wondered for a moment to which of them he referred. But James was as blandly ambiguous as ever, his face betraying nothing but brotherly consideration. She stared at him coldly, and wordlessly turned on her heel and walked away.

James remained for a long time, drawing upon one of his favourite black cigars, while his brain worked as smoothly as an oiled machine, selecting, discarding, planning for the future. Albert's death was as unfortunate as it was unexpected, but there was one saving grace: Albert's plans would not die with him, other hands would take over and the four steamships would be built according to their original specifications. Fogarty's hash had been settled. James blew out a cloud of smoke and dismissed him as an incompetent romantic fool. Then there was his own marriage to consider. All was arranged. The future looked quite rosy. There was nothing that could go wrong. He had planned for every eventuality.

Leonora sat up in the broad marital bed, shook out her chestnut hair, and smiled fondly at Richard.

'You know how dear Papa so longs for a grandson?'

'I should,' said Richard. 'For he has done little else but remind me of the fact.'

'Dear Papa,' whispered Leonora softly, 'is so intemperate of character that it would not do to disappoint him.' She looked slyly at Richard. 'As for you, sir, you are rebuked.'

'Me?'

'For wasting time, Mr Onedin. A great deal of precious time.'

Richard made due acknowledgment of his error and blew out the light.